NO LONGER PROPERTY
SEATTLE PUBLIC LIBRARY

Advance Praise for ***Still Life with Monkey***

"Weber's genius in these startling, haunting stories is to find the momentary connections in things that make up or derail a life, be it an artichoke and a dead woman's earrings, or a plant and a hospice worker. Written in prose as dazzling and finecrafted as diamonds, Weber's stories show us ordinary people in extraordinary moments, doing what the best literature does—they make us look at our own world differently." —**Caroline Leavitt, author of** *Pictures of You* **and** *Cruel Beautiful World*

"With eloquence, wit, and wisdom, Katharine Weber transports her readers from Madagascar to Connecticut, from jury duty to a feast of poisonous mushrooms. In the best way, I never knew what I would find on the next page in this wonderfully engaging, vividly peopled collection." —**Margot Livesey, author of** *The Boy in the Field* **and** *The Hidden Machinery*

"Katharine Weber's trademark intelligence and wit are on full, dazzling display in her not-to-be missed, career-spanning collection. Secret family histories, childhood games turned dangerous, moments imbued with fierce, unexpected consequences, inform these compulsively readable, razor-sharp stories. A triumph." —**Kate Walbert, author of** *She Was Like That* **and** *His Favorites*

"Weber's sly, elegant stories unfurl to reveal themselves from inside out, startlingly beautiful, sharp-edged, funny, and moving. This collection is sheer pleasure to read." —**Kate Christensen, PEN/Faulkner award-winning author of** *The Great Man* **and** *The Last Cruise*

"Whether she's turning her attention to the miniature tragedy of a group of curious neighborhood girls at play among dangerous chemicals, uncovering new details of the grand harrowing European Jewish experience in WWII, or simply giving us a glimpse of a fraught relationship on a trip to Geneva, Katharine Weber's linked stories are always full of her signature verve, subtle wit, and precision. This is an impressive collection of interwoven stories, marked by breadth, fierce intelligence, and sheer storytelling talent." —**Daniel Torday, author of** *Boomer1* **and** *The Last Flight of Poxl West*

Praise for Katharine Weber's Previous Books

STILL LIFE WITH MONKEY

"Stark and compelling . . . Rigorously unsentimental yet suffused with emotion: possibly the best work yet from an always stimulating writer." —*Kirkus Reviews* (starred review)

"In precise and often luminous prose, with intelligence and tenderness, Weber's latest novel examines the question of what makes a life worth living." —*Washington Post*

"[A] deeply but delicately penetrating novel." —*New York Times Book Review*

"Weber's unsentimental and poignant examination of what does and does not make life worth living is a heartbreaking triumph." —*Publishers Weekly* (starred review)

"Radiantly tender and piercingly sad. Katharine Weber is a magician of a novelist, one who writes about loss and loneliness with such compassion and humor that we feel enchanted as we read." —Brian Morton, author of *Starting Out in the Evening*

"A brilliantly crafted novel, brimming with heart." —Tayari Jones, author of *An American Marriage*

TRUE CONFECTIONS

"[A] sly and playful book . . . *True Confections* is a hoot, but a hoot with an edge." —*Cleveland Plain Dealer*

"[S]ucculently inventive . . . A novel should give us 'that unique blend of sweetness and pleasure and something else, a deep note of something rich and exotic and familiar' that a bite of good chocolate does. *True Confections* certainly delivers that delectability." —*Washington Post Book World*

"Wickedly funny . . . sly and engrossing." —Jennifer Reese, *NPR Book Review*

TRIANGLE

"A thing of beauty . . . a structurally dazzling novel whose formal acrobatics have a purpose beyond their own cleverness."
—Maureen Corrigan, NPR's *Fresh Air*

"Katharine Weber's crackerjack historical mystery may be the most effective 9/11 novel yet written— and it isn't even about 9/11." —*Entertainment Weekly*

"A haunting exercise in memory." —*New York Magazine*

THE LITTLE WOMEN

"Stops being droll only to be funny and almost never stops being exceedingly smart." —Richard Eder, *New York Times*

THE MUSIC LESSON

"As intricate as an acrostic . . . Weber's skill is such that her puzzle engages the reader's attention throughout." —*The New Yorker*

"[A]ffecting and elegant." —*The New York Times Book Review*

"Wonderful . . . a super book that tells a dynamic and tightly controlled story, in prose sensual with the smell of things, the feel of things . . . genuinely surprising." —Kate Atkinson

OBJECTS IN MIRROR ARE CLOSER THAN THEY APPEAR

"With vibrancy and a steady barrage of linguistic brio . . . Weber provides a blend of artistry and insight far beyond what we usually see in a first novel." —*San Francisco Chronicle*

"Katharine Weber, in her stunning first novel, might be a murder-mystery author, so tight is her style as she examines four lives and their effect on each other, seeing each one as if in mirrors which do not tell the truth—a fascinating read." —May Sarton

"An amazing first novel . . . It is wise, flippant, deep, witty—characteristics which are seldom found together. It is also a good story, and Harriet Rose is a marvelous and endearing character."
—Madeleine L'Engle

"I much enjoyed this delightfully witty novel." —Iris Murdoch

Jane of Hearts

AND OTHER STORIES

ALSO BY KATHARINE WEBER

Still Life with Monkey
The Memory of All That
True Confections
Triangle
The Little Women
The Music Lesson
Objects in Mirror Are Closer Than They Appear

JANE
of
HEARTS

AND OTHER STORIES

Katharine Weber

PAUL DRY BOOKS
Philadelphia 2022

First Paul Dry Books Edition, 2022

Paul Dry Books, Inc.
Philadelphia, Pennsylvania
www.pauldrybooks.com

Copyright © 2022 Katharine Weber
All rights reserved

Printed in the United States of America

Library of Congress Control Number: 2021948286
ISBN 978-1-58988-159-4

Credits appear on page 204

For my beloved Smith men—
Wilder, Beau, and Robbie

Contents

Jane of Hearts

AND OTHER STORIES

Mr. Antler's Princess Dust

It was the summer they tried going door to door selling poison mushrooms. Barbara Antler lived across the alley. She was only a few months younger than Harriet Rose, really almost the same age but, being in fourth grade, a year ahead, Harriet made all the decisions. Barbara's little sister Debbie, a bulky four-year-old who sucked her thumb, was theirs to do with as they pleased.

Debbie still rode Barbara's cast-off pink bicycle with crooked training wheels. It listed to one side; she had learned to ride it by counterbalancing all of her weight the other way in order not to tip over. Harriet thought that it would probably take Debbie a million years to learn to ride a normal bicycle.

Harriet and Barbara left her behind the day they sold the mushrooms. They appropriated her wagon, though, dumping doll passengers in an unceremonious Jonestown-ish driveway heap before setting off to harvest the toadstools and fungi that sprouted in the moist summer heat on lawns and under trees and hedges here and there in the neighborhood.

By the time their meandering path had taken them several streets away, Harriet and Barbara were filthy, and they had amassed a sufficient stock to begin selling. Neither of them knew whose idea this enterprise was; between them the notion had sprouted as spontaneously as the glistening fungus for which they foraged.

It was astonishingly easy to sell their produce. In preparation, they smudged their faces with their dirty hands in order to look like the poor Gypsy children in Harriet's old Secret Seven books that had been her mother's. They wrapped t-shirts on their heads in vague approximations of exotic babushkas.

Harriet approached the first house, rang the bell, and when the door opened she drew a long breath and launched into the sales pitch, though she couldn't see more than the folded arms of the lady who stood behind the blurry screened door. She deployed what she hoped was a convincingly foreign-sounding accent, while Barbara stayed by their toadstool wagon at the foot of the steps, shyly proffering their finest specimens in a mute appeal.

"Hey lady, you like my special deluxe mushrooms, special today, freshly picked?"

After a momentary pause, the lady murmured "Oh dear, oh my," and ran to get her money. She gave them all she had in the house, four dollars, which bought her a special deluxe assortment of sixteen of their largest, finest fungi, including their only puffball. The man at the next house seemed equally anxious to acquire the mushrooms, for which he unquestioningly met the asking price of twenty-five cents apiece. They were sold out. They were rich.

By the time Harriet and Barbara came home, having trailed the sound of the Good Humor man for a few blocks until they found him, and having spent some of their profits on toasted almond bars—two each—Mrs. Antler was furious. There had been telephone calls. Harriet's parents weren't home yet, but they would hear about this soon enough. Did Barbara and Harriet know the mushrooms were probably poisonous? Had they eaten any? Had it occurred to them that if anybody ate those mushrooms something terrible could have happened? Did they know that those nice people had given them money in exchange for the nasty objects in order to prevent possible tragedy? Did they know what it was going to be like to spend the rest of the week grounded, limited to their own backyards, thinking about the danger of playing with poison?

Debbie was unbearably agreeable, so they spent the next day trying to get her to eat things. Mrs. Antler opened her front door on this particular July morning and thrust Debbie out onto the stoop around mid-morning. "You big girls play with Debbie! Be nice!" she called to Harriet and Barbara, who were on their knees violently chalking the front walk in raging boredom. The door slammed shut. Debbie jammed her thumb into her mouth and sat down on the top step, eying the girls.

"Do you want to play restaurant, Deb?" Harriet and Barbara chorused together. She nodded her head yes without removing the thumb. Her eyes were wide with her usual amiable apprehension. Harriet, an only child, could never figure out why Debbie rarely resisted their schemes despite the inevitable humiliations. She would eat anything. They ground their chalk stubs into the bricks until there was nothing but powder.

Out of a paper cup Debbie drank milk and orange juice mixed together into a slurry with the chalk powder. She ate cream cheese spread on stale saltines Mrs. Antler had thrown away because of ants in the box. Harriet and Barbara mixed snot in with the cream cheese and spread it on an anty saltine, and Debbie ate that one, too.

For Zee Next Course they chopped up desiccated spiders from the Roses' cellar and mixed them with Hawaiian Punch. This was served to Debbie in a tall plastic tumbler on a plate, which Harriet presented with a sommelier's flourish, a dish towel draped over one arm. Debbie sat contentedly on the stoop and drank it all in one prolonged gulp. She wiped her stained mouth and asked if there was any more. Harriet and Barbara laughed and laughed until Barbara actually wet her pants and had to run into her house to change with her hands clamped between her legs.

Bored with waiting for Barbara to come back outside, Harriet got up and signaled for Debbie to follow her to her own backyard.

"Can you climb?" Harriet demanded of Debbie. Debbie nodded. Harriet began to climb the rose trellis that was built against the brick wall that divided the Roses' backyard from the alley. The two girls crawled along the top of the wall to the end, where it ran into the side of the Antlers' garage. Standing up and stretching to reach, Harriet grabbed the ornamental wooden railing that ran around the garage roof, which was otherwise flat. She pulled herself up and then climbed over the railing to the top of the garage. She reached down for Debbie's hand and hauled her up to the edge, where Debbie could get a foothold and clamber over the railing on her own.

Mr. Antler had expressly forbidden the children to climb on the garage. The roof, he said, wouldn't support their weight. He was wrong. Harriet heard a tapping sound and turned toward it. Barbara was at her bedroom window on the second floor. The second story was much closer than usual from up here. She was gesturing with some urgency and pointing down toward the driveway. Harriet couldn't make out what she was mouthing, but then understood as she recognized the sound of Mr. Antler's car.

There was no time to climb down so Harriet flattened herself like a soldier under fire and waved furiously at Debbie to do likewise. They could hear Mr. Antler's car stop. His car door opened and closed.

Harriet wiggled over the tarry rooftop to the front edge and peered through the wooden railing. She could see the top of his baseball cap. He was standing stock still in front of his beloved rose trellis. He often stood around like that. Harriet remembered hearing her father say to her mother, when they drove past the Antlers' house once and Albert Antler was standing on his front lawn, "There he is. Lord and master of all that he surveys."

"What's my father doing?" whispered Debbie.

Harriet crept back to the middle of the roof. Her hands were black with something. She looked down. So were her knees. Her shirt had grey skid marks down the front.

"Surveying."

"Oh."

Together they both crept back to the edge of the roof. It was hot, and the close-up smell of tar was a little sickening. Harriet raised her head to peek through the railing again. Mr. Antler was taking bags out of the trunk of his car. He was grunting with the effort. He stopped suddenly and looked up. Harriet had a piercing, thrilling sense that he was looking right at her. It was all over. They would be in trouble. After the poison mushrooms, Barbara might be forbidden to play with Harriet altogether. But now he was walking toward the garage. He was right under them. He didn't know they were there. Harriet ducked down and pushed Debbie's head down.

They could hear the garage door creak open. The Antlers' garage door was the old kind that was suspended on a track and rolled sideways. Mr. Antler came out of his garage a moment later behind his garden cart. Harriet and Debbie were there for so long, baking in the sun with the roof tar and listening to the sounds of Mr. Antler going back and forth with his cart, that Harriet almost fell asleep. The sound of the garage door sliding closed roused her. Neither girl moved until they heard the Antlers' back door crashing shut. Then they crept over to the edge of the roof, scaled down the side to the trellis, avoiding thorns, and jumped down into the Antlers' yard, where Barbara was waiting.

"You can't play with us anymore," Barbara said to Debbie. "Go away."

"I'll tell," Debbie said around her thumb.

"If you do then I'll pinch you without making a mark."

"I'll tell about that too," said Debbie, enunciating carefully around the thumb.

"You'll be sorry," Barbara threatened automatically.

"Forget it. She can play with us," interrupted Harriet with impatience. "What's in the bags your father put in the garage?"

The Antler children knew how to roll open the garage door quietly. Mr. Antler, according to Barbara, was probably making his shower drink and then would be in the bathroom for a safe while.

"Blue shins," Debbie chimed in.

"What?" Harriet was intrigued. It was the sort of Antler thing that fascinated her, like the way the Antler children wore "guest pajamas" when their parents entertained.

"He does his blue shins," Barbara explained. "Maybe he shaves them. I know it's something like that."

Inside the garage, they rolled the door nearly closed again. The bags were stacked in neat piles in one corner.

"What does L-I-M-" began Debbie, standing with her head turned sideways so she could read the lettering on the top bag.

"Lime, dummy," interrupted Barbara. "He puts it on the lawn. And then there's manure, yuck."

"What's eyo-eyo-eyo?" asked Debbie, still reading from the bags.

"What?" Harriet hadn't expected Debbie to be able to read this well.

"Oh, jerk, that's 10-10-10 fertilizer," Barbara answered self-importantly. "He told me about that. The numbers mean how much of different things there are in it. Like nitrogen and fluoride."

"Chore—Chlordane," read Harriet from the smallest bag that lay apart from the other heavier sacks. Barbara picked it up and carried it over to the crack of light that filtered in from the doorway. The bag was surprisingly light. They tried to read the tiny print on the side but it was mostly directions for application. There was a string stitched across the top of the bag. Barbara pulled it open. Inside was the most beautiful pink glitter.

"Debbie, come here a sec," Harriet beckoned. "Would you like to be a fairy princess?"

"Yes." Still with the thumb.

"Would you eat the magic potion so you could be a fairy princess?"

"Yes."

Harriet's gaze met Barbara's over the top of Debbie's head.

"This way, your soon-to-be Royal Highness," said Barbara, sweeping her arms wide and speaking in a deferential tone. Debbie, only slightly suspicious, drifted after her out into the sunshine.

Barbara ambushed her beside the yew bushes at Harriet's signal. She covered Debbie's mouth with one hand, twisted one of her sister's pudgy arms behind her, and propelled the reluctantly cooperative prisoner forward.

"It's part of the game, it's part of the game," soothed Harriet behind them. "You can't turn into a princess until you've been held captive, and then rescued by a handsome prince," she added logically.

Debbie nodded, and Barbara took her hand away from Debbie's mouth. The thumb went back in. Barbara wiped her hand on her shorts.

Harriet went off to the Antlers' side yard where she began to strip the yew bushes of their red berries, which she dropped into a bucket from the Antlers' sand box.

Plink, plank, plunk, she thought. Poisonberries for Debbie. The berries were plump, pimiento-red, and had small green recessed centers. They looked like inside-out versions of the stuffed olives her mother served in a bowl with drinks.

When she had about two dozen, Harriet began to mash them with a bent spoon she had salvaged from an Antler flower bed months before. (She suspected that Mrs. Antler had missed it, since it had a complicated pattern of flowers twined around a very fancy "A" on the end. Debbie must have taken it outside, or it had been dropped at a cocktail party.)

Barbara, meanwhile, led Debbie down the outside steps to the cellar door, where an abandoned milk crate sat in a swirl of windblown leaves from the previous fall. There she seated the one who aspired to royal status. Debbie was docile while Barbara bound her wrists behind her with an old jump rope.

"Wait here. No noise or you're out."

Debbie nodded, her lips compressed tightly.

Barbara skipped up the steps to find Harriet, who approached with the bucket in one hand and the bag of pink glitter under her other arm.

Barbara took the bucket. They marched in a grand procession of two down the steps toward Debbie, who sat motionless on the milk crate.

"I, the royal prince, have come to rescue you, fair maiden," intoned Harriet. "You must eat this tasty potion and your bonds shall fall asunder."

Barbara began to undo the big loose knots that held Debbie's wrists. Harriet dipped the spoon into the berry mash and scraped up a tiny helping. She lifted it to Debbie's slightly parted lips.

Barbara yanked the jump rope free at the same moment. As Debbie's face crumpled up, Harriet felt a stab of worry. Had she actually been poisoned? No, the rope bindings had burned Debbie's soft wrists.

"Don't cry! You're a princess!" Harriet shouted, dipping both hands into the bag of pink glitter that lay open at her feet. She threw a double handful into the air.

"You're a princess!" shouted Barbara, heaving a fistful of the magic dust straight up over their heads.

"We're all princesses," shouted Harriet, throwing another double handful up into the air around them. "The world is a princess!" The three girls ran up the steps together, Harriet carrying the magic dust. They reached into the bag, throwing up handful after handful.

Princess dust rained down on their heads and arms and formed a soft pink mist that drifted in all directions. For a sparkling instant, the kingdom of the Antlers' backyard was the most beautiful place on earth.

Friend of the Family

Well, Benedict,

A trout with its tail in its mouth. On a plate. Before me. It's called Truite au Bleu, and Victor insisted that I have it, that it was my obligation as a visitor to Geneva to have it, and so I did, but disconcerting as that was—do you know they boil them alive?—it paled beside the disconcertingness of attempting to dine in public with Anne and Victor.

Since I got here, three days ago, I've been feeling that I must have missed the first act. Where is the Anne Gordon with whom I lived in New York, happily, for more than a year in those two rooms on Eighth Street? Her letters didn't prepare me for this transformation. Her rhapsodies about the glories of Victor didn't prepare me for a balding Hungarian refugee more than twice her age. A married one, with three children. In just six months Our Lady of the Perpetual Milk Crate has evolved into I don't quite know what: a chic, jaded mistress person. Anne of Cleavage.

She has a very grownup modern flat, and this Victor about whom I have heard so much (and about whom I now realize I knew nothing) turns out to be, creepily, Anne's boss at U.G.P. (That solves the mystery of how Anne, working in the back room at the Shippen Gallery on Madison Avenue, was recruited by a Swiss oil broker, or whatever it is that U.G.P.

is and does.) Victor is a "friend of the family," and has known Anne since she was little. Anne has reminded me that I did once meet him, when he came to pick her up at Eighth Street for dinner. I guess I vaguely recall some guy in a blazer, one of dozens of people from Eastern Europe who constitute a large group known to Anne as "friends of the family," standing in our hallway, winded after three flights of stairs. It didn't occur to me to notice him. It didn't occur to me in all these months that *that* was Victor. He even *looks* like "Daddy" (a dour Hungarian baker with a flour allergy who lives alone with his bitter memories in deepest New Jersey), whose life Victor is credited with saving in a children's barracks (where they shared a bunk) at Auschwitz. Something about a potato.

To get to dinner, Anne and I took a bus to the outskirts of Geneva, and then walked for nearly a mile along a somewhat barren avenue where, believe me, nobody ordinarily walks. Anne had to walk in front of me because the traffic was so alarmingly close that walking together would have been dangerous. As it was, I thought it was dangerous. We picked our way along the shoulder of this road that was like a suburban Riverside Drive. Cars would rush past us, and I would feel the force of air pushing me, pulling me. Anne's skirt would swirl up. She has great legs. Walking a few paces behind her afforded me the same view that strangers in passing cars were getting.

There was something oddly seductive about her; she has a new walk that somehow exaggerates her femaleness in an almost cartoonish way. Is this how a mistress walks? She has very high-heeled strappy sandals. She walks very fast. I felt as though, compared to her, I was a sexless companion, like a dog or an old nanny, lumbering along faithfully behind her, steady as she goes. And I was wearing the blue sundress you like, which you always say looks so good with a bit of a tan. And let me tell you, I have quite a lot more tan than I meant to, because of yesterday's bizarre lake adventure.

Yesterday: Victor turned up unexpectedly, as Sundays are usually his family day, when Anne does things like bleach her mustache and (very painfully) wax her thighs. Anne had, in fact, spoken of such activities, but was, luckily, languishing over a piece of toast when the downstairs buzzer sounded with Victor's specially coded three shorts and one long. (Mrs. Beethoven: "What, Ludwig, me inspire you? Ha Ha Ha Haa!")

Victor had been set free, he explained after an awfully long, silent greeting at the door; I kept my gaze tactfully averted while he and Anne did whatever it is that they do, with more passion than anyone else has ever experienced in the history of humankind. Victor's wife, Annamarie, had taken the children—who are called Lucien, Otto, and Minerva, if you can believe it—to the beach. As everyone apparently knows, Victor does not like going to the beach, for reasons that will be revealed presently.

Anne, who can be maddeningly passive in her dealings with Victor (how can this be Anne, the least accommodating person I have ever known; just try to argue with her about the pronunciation of *forte* or *banal*, just try to get her to go in the main entrance of the Metropolitan instead of her beloved Eighty-first Street side entrance for the cognoscenti), surprised me when she began to pout about how *she* never gets to go to the beach, how she should have rung up Annamarie (she has dinner there from time to time, and has baby-sat for them on three occasions) and finagled an invitation to join them if she had only known. (What beach, you might well ask. Some lakeside resort or other, with sandy beaches.)

I think she surprised Victor, too. He thought, perhaps, that he was calling her bluff when he said, "Oh, very well then, we go to the beach. Get your things. A towel. I cannot swim, though, because I have no swimming costume."

He sat at Anne's table with his hands placed palms up before him, as though he were old and weary and unable to do anything but acquiesce.

"We can buy you a suit at the chemist's on the corner—I've seen them there," Anne said. Victor looked helplessly at me. I didn't know what he wanted me to say. I remember when Anne patronized mere drugstores.

"You two should go," I began.

"No!" they chorused.

"I take so much of Anne's time from you, and you are her closest friend—it wouldn't be right to keep her for the whole Sunday," Victor said.

"There isn't much privacy at a beach anyway," Anne pointed out, as if this were a practical observation. (They weren't going to fuck anyway? Something about this remark highlighted the illicit point of this whole alliance. It felt loaded with some sort of beyond obvious sexual *je ne sais quoi* I haven't grasped yet.)

So Victor's swim togs were acquired, and we were all heading off in his white Citroën toward some beach. What if we were to run into Victor's family, I inquired mildly from the back seat. I never know if it's O.K. to bring them up or not.

"We go to France," Victor says over his shoulder as he drives too fast down an access ramp and onto a highway without pausing, which causes the BMW closing in behind us in the near lane to swerve around the Citroën with a blaring horn and an obscene gesture from the driver.

"Nazi!" hisses Victor, who speeds up.

Anne puts her hand on his arm, and we drop back. "He had Stuttgart plates," she explains to me, turning her head so she can see me. I feel as though I'm out with somebody's parents.

I didn't have my passport with me, but Victor assured me that no one would check at the border, and he was right; we were waved through, Victor's white Citroën looking like an ambulance racing toward the scene of an accident. I'm in another country, I thought. I'm in France.

The lake was near the border, and we were there in minutes. For someone who doesn't swim, Victor seemed surprisingly well-informed about the whereabouts of this beach, where the parking lot was situated, where to change, and where the cold-drinks stand was.

We changed in a wooden shack. Victor went in after we came out (I feeling particularly thigh-conscious in my old black bathing suit; Anne looking terrific in a black bikini I would never have known her to wear in her former life), and emerged wearing his new swim trunks, his office-y white button-down shirt open. The swim trunks were an imitation-Hawaiian print that was like canned laughter. He was wearing his dark socks and thick-soled leather shoes. His legs were somehow pathetic and birdlike. The rest of him seemed more commanding and intense. I felt embarrassed for him when I glanced at his hairless shins.

We aligned ourselves on the sand with Anne between us. Victor took off his shoes and socks, and his shirt, which he folded into a fussy square for a pillow. Victor and Anne lay face down on their towels, with fingers linked. They both turned their heads away from me. I think their eyes were closed. The sun glittered off Anne's new (to me) diamond earring. (Victor could hardly give her a ring, she had explained.) I had the feeling that all the other people there knew what they wanted to do. I felt alone. I missed you, I wanted to have someone with me, too, so I wouldn't be the third wheel, and I hadn't brought a book. Damn. I sat up on my towel.

Nobody was swimming. It wasn't very hot. There were only a few other people around; no children at all. A woman several yards from us was sunbathing with the top of her suit pulled down to her waist. The woman sat very upright, partially facing in our direction in order to catch every ray of the sun, with her legs straight out in front of her. The posture emphasized her potbelly, and her nipples were like a second pair of eyes looking at me. I regretted the decision to leave my camera in the flat. I felt her glaring at me and realized I had been staring. I was glad I had left my camera in the flat.

I began to dig in the dry sand with one hand. I scrabbled

out a rather large ditch that described the arc my arm could swing through freely without my changing position. I felt something under my fingers. It was a white plastic tampon applicator.

"A beach whistle," I observed to Anne, who had turned her head my way. She wrinkled her nose in distaste. I buried it near my feet, where I wouldn't disturb it again. Either these beachgoers were unusually tidy or the French comb this beach regularly, because there was very little interesting detritus. I would have expected to find Gauloise butts galore. I felt the edge of a shell as I was reinserting the tampon applicator in the sand. I examined the shell. It was nearly flat, somewhat oval, a thin yellow bit of translucency. It reminded me of the sort I used to find on the beach the summer I was six, when I spent two months with my mother and grandmother in Cornwall; it's a kind of shell I haven't seen since.

"Toenail, anyone?" I said, offering my find to Anne.

"Shut up, will you?" she said to me with surprising intensity. Was this a No Talking beach? I had no idea what the problem was.

"Yes, please, I would like a toenail," came Victor's voice. I had thought he was asleep. His head was still turned away. "Hello. I ordered the toenail. Make that ten. Could you deliver them right away?" This wasn't Victor's style, that I knew of. Maybe he kidded around much more with Anne when I wasn't there. I was momentarily confused.

"Here's one," I said, holding the shell out to him over Anne's head. She had lain back down on her towel and was squeezing her eyes tight shut. Nobody moved. My arm was still extended over Anne. Her back heaved, and I realized she was suppressing sobs. Victor's head was still turned away. His voice was weirdly disembodied.

"Don't you have them ready for me?" he said languidly. I still didn't get it.

He rolled over and sat up.

"Anne is now upset with both of us," he announced. "She is upset with you for bringing up a bad subject. You did not know. She is upset with me for playing my little game with you. Isn't that right?"

Victor patted the top of Anne's head and stroked her shoulders. Something about her tears seemed to please him. He was now sitting up in the same doll-like position as the topless woman on my right. I saw his feet.

Benedict, I know human flesh cannot melt, but what I saw looked like the melted stubs of feet. Victor has no toes. They froze off at Auschwitz. The Allied doctors wanted to amputate his feet, but he wouldn't let them. (Anne told me all this when Victor went to get us cold drinks a little while later.)

The Pobble grinned at me. He saw me seeing his feet. I did not like his delight in my discomfort, in Anne's anguish.

"I'm sorry," I said, meeting his gaze.

"Of course you are," he said, rather nastily, I thought.

"Of course you wouldn't like to swim," sobbed Anne. "I didn't think."

"Of course you didn't, my pet," said Victor, smiling a cold smile.

We had been at the lake for about an hour, and we stayed there, more or less in silence, for another hour. It felt necessary to sit there so it wouldn't be the upsetting discussion that made us leave, even though I doubt that I was the only one who felt like bolting for the Citroën. While Victor fetched Perriers with straws, and the Belgian mocha biscuits that he considers superior to all other forms of cookie life, Anne told me the story of Victor's toes, gazing out at the lake the whole time. I found myself imagining their sex life being somehow profoundly affected by this absence. What does he have her do to make up for it? As Victor struggled across the sand carrying the mineral water and the biscuits, I had to avoid studying his gait. He put on his shoes and socks for the short walk.

I wondered if his shoes had special toe weights that helped him walk. Even the sight of his fingers gripping the necks of the Perrier bottles was mildly surprising. I wondered if his toes had looked like his fingers. I curled and uncurled my toes uncomfortably.

The drive back to Geneva was mostly silent. We all three of us had terrible sunburns.

"*Merde*," muttered Anne when she was through studying herself in Victor's rearview mirror. (I was relieved when she was finished, as I thought he might want to have the use of it on the highway.) "In the office tomorrow, how do we explain matching sunburns?"

"I went to the beach with my family, and you went to a different beach with your visiting friend," Victor answered. "Thousands of people went to the beach today. Why worry about the coincidence of it?"

What a shit, I thought. A charming shit. With a sunburn. And no toes.

I'm sorry, Benedict, how did we get here? Right: Anne and I were walking along the side of the road on our way to the trout restaurant, she with her skirt flying and her sexy legs, I with my sunburn and in the blue dress you like. Anne had just reported over her shoulder that we were nearly there when a car skidded onto the gravel in front of us, giving me a serious scare. It was Victor's white Citroën.

"Would you like a ride?"

Anne played it as if he were a stranger. "No, thanks anyway. *Merci, non.*"

Victor waggled his eyebrows at me. I shrugged.

"Very well, ladies. *Ciao.*" He drove off. I could see his taillight flash about a quarter mile up the road, and then the Citroën turned right and was lost from sight.

"It's better to arrive separately, in case anyone's there," she said over her shoulder.

"Anyone?"

"Any friend of Annamarie's. Any friend of the family."

"You're a friend of the family."

"Don't be dense," she said reprovingly. "It would be a disaster." She lingered over the word "disaster" the way some people savor the words "*foie gras.*"

Although the Citroën had been in the parking lot for ten minutes by the time we approached the maître d's pulpit, Victor was nowhere in evidence.

"We have a reservation for three?" Anne said in French. "The name is Goldfarb."

We were shown to a table in an elegant garden courtyard. It was early by Swiss standards, and we were the first customers of the evening. There were only five or six tables, all covered to the ground with snowy tablecloths, and very widely spaced across the white gravel courtyard. The tables were all big enough to seat eight or ten people. Ours had three place settings, at noon, four, and eight.

Anne and I picked up two wineglasses and moved together in the direction of the third. We sat down, leaving a place for Victor between us. This might seem like a small thing, but moments like that are what our friendship thrives on, has driven on, that in-synch, "two thoughts with but a single mind" kind of instant, commonplace when we were roommates in New York but so rare since I've been here that I made a mental note of it.

A flurry of Bemelmans waiters rushed to rearrange the place settings. (What we had done was very naughty.) There was a stream running by, only a few feet from us, and the noise of it meant that we had to raise our voices slightly to converse, even after our rearrangement.

"So typical," said Anne. "So Swiss to seat us that way—so we use the table completely—with no thought to conversational distances."

"Or something. Maybe they don't like the idea of private conversations," I suggested. "And who is Goldfarb?"

"I thought you knew."

"Do I?" Did I?

"It was my father's father's name. Daddy changed it."

"Why?"

"Anti-Semitism, I suppose."

I thought of an imperious dowager of Scottish ancestry (and proud of it) called Peggy Gordon. I once heard her say to my grandmother, Gay, that she thought half the Gordons in New York were Jews who had changed their names from Goldfarb, Goldstein, and so on. "Why can't they just change it to Gold?" Peggy asked plaintively. "It's shorter and nearer, but you can still tell. I would rather expect them to like a nice, glittering name like Gold."

Gay had laughed and offered her more to drink. I thought, from my vantage point in Gay's bedroom, where I was sorting out all her jewelry on her bedspread—I must have been about ten—that her laugh was not so much with Peggy as at her. There was also my own parentage to consider. I was not only Gay Gibson's granddaughter, I was Simon Rose's daughter. I wonder now whether Peggy Gordon ever considered for one second that her words could hurt me, could hurt my feelings. Doubtful. It probably didn't occur to her that I thought of myself as Jewish. She always fussed over me because I looked so much like a Gibson. I had "the Gibson upper lip."

Gay was fond of her because they went back a long way, and had traveled to Reno together for their first divorces. By the time I was six I knew that the Truckee River ran through Reno, where you went for a divorce. You stood on a bridge and threw your now meaningless wedding ring into that river.

Once, when I was little, the people next door, the Antlers, had a terrible argument, and Mrs. Antler ran out the front door and threw her wedding ring into the bushes in front of their house. I saw her do it. That night I watched from my bedroom window as Mr. and Mrs. Antler together hunted through those bushes, on their knees, with flashlights, for hours.

So, Benedict, where I come from there were a lot of wedding rings tossed around. Me, when I have a wedding ring, I don't intend to take it off. Ever. Just so you know.

Victor sidled into the courtyard just when the waiter was presenting us with menus as big as the bonnet of a small car. Victor joined us, and the waiter nearly knocked off Victor's reading glasses as he flourished another menu under his nose. We were each hidden from sight behind this menu flotilla. Everything about this place was slightly oversized. Perhaps that signifies luxury. I imagine that we looked, from above, like three giant moths poised for flight.

The voice of Victor insisted that I order the Truite au Bleu, the specialty of the place. He ordered gray sole for Anne, who contributed no thoughts of her own about what she would like to eat.

"I will take the steak," he said to the waiter—rather imperiously, I thought. Why did it bother me so? "I will take the steak." I have no toes, so I will not merely have, as others do, but I will take. I survived childhood at Auschwitz, so I can cheat on my wife and I will take the steak.

The waiter plucked away the menus. I cannot begin to enumerate all the ways that I do not like this man. I do not like what Anne has become, is becoming, will become. A spinster with a special feeling for a certain flower stall. (Victor bought her flowers there once; she has taken me to see the particular shade of roses this vendor sells, and I was made to admire them as if the very shade of pink signals the deep significance of it all.) A childless woman alone on holidays. A woman with a gray soul.

Why did I expect that Anne would pay for this meal? In fact, in the end she did pick up the check, but not because

Victor managed the simple maneuver of looking the other way. No, by the time the check came it was much more complicated than that.

Our starters had been served, consumed, and cleared (duck-liver pâté and vegetable terrine, quite good, actually, though Victor had been unpleasant with the waiter's suggestion that he might like soup—thoughtless of the waiter not to realize that, having lived on ghastly soup in a concentration camp, Victor is greatly pained when soup possibilities arise in his present life) when another group was seated across from us.

At this point Anne was seated between Victor and me; when Victor was shown to our table, Anne had moved over nearer to me, either despite or in response to Victor's murmured, "Ah, I shall be a thorn between two roses." So we had got ourselves into the same configuration as at the beach. I thought I saw Victor looking uncomfortable, but I didn't think it was in response to anything said, as our conversation at that juncture was pointless and desultory, mostly about the food. The next time I turned my head Victor had disappeared.

He had simply vanished. Anne looked quite disturbed.

"What happened to Victor?" I felt, for a brief moment, on the edge of hysteria, like Ingrid Bergman in "Gaslight." I also had an absurd sense that Anne was about to launch into a complete summary of What Happened to Victor, up to and including the Allied doctors wanting to amputate those hideous feet. Was Victor a demon? A golem? I wished I had taken his picture.

"Victor is right here—he's under the table," Anne murmured, looking straight ahead, her lips barely moving. Her tension was almost comical. I half expected her to say, "Just act natural."

"May I ask why?"

"A woman who plays tennis with Annamarie is at that table."

"Ah. An F. of the F."

"Don't—this is serious," Anne ground out at me through clenched teeth. There was a muffled gasp from under our table. In an attempt to kick me, she had kicked Victor.

Our main courses arrived, borne out to the courtyard by three waiters in a procession. Each carried a tray on which was a plate under a silver dome. The domed plates were placed before us. Victor's was set down at his place. The three waiters looked confused.

"*Monsieur?*" one murmured.

"Monsieur had to leave," Anne replied, in English, so indistinctly that the waiter almost couldn't hear her over the rushing of the stream. He cupped his hand behind one ear and bent down over her shoulder.

"Is everything all right, Mademoiselle?" he asked, also switching to English.

"*Oui*," she answered, cutting off any further discussion.

"You can leave the steak," I said, figuring that Victor might still want to eat it somehow. Also, we were going to have to pay for it. Hell, I would take it home and eat it.

The waiters glumly went through their ritual of simultaneous revelation, whisking all three silver domes high into the air after a wordless count of three. Victor's absence had spoiled it for them.

Now what?

Anne and I ate dinner in total silence. One of her hands was in her lap all through the meal; I realized that she must be stroking Victor's head or something.

"Look, does this happen a lot?"

She shook her head, giving me reason to believe that it did and that discussion about it was unwelcome at this time. I didn't know whether to hurry or linger over the food. How were we going to get Victor out of there unseen? I poked at my trout, which stared me down. I ate my potatoes and my courgette matchsticks done up in a bundle and tied with a string of chive.

My few days in Geneva with Anne had seemed beyond ordinary experience from the start, but this evening was now taking on aspects of a de Chirico. The waiters, the artificial outdoor setting, the imitation of gracious service, the contrived arrangements of food, the deception of Anne's true love lurking under the tablecloth—nothing seemed real. The food had no taste in my mouth. The wine, a Gewürz, tasted like glass.

Across from us, the waiter was erecting menus in front of the people at the table with Annamarie's tennis friend, and, when he had worked his way around, their view in our direction was completely obscured. Victor must have been on the lookout for this opportunity; he flung the tablecloth up and bolted straight out like a sprinter crouched at the starting block when the gun goes off.

Anne and I sat very still, as if we had agreed in advance to ignore this moment. Without turning my head I saw the edge of Victor's jacket go by, and I could hear for an instant the crunching of Victor's shoes on gravel; perhaps I only thought I could hear the Citroën engine turn over. The escape from Stalag 17 was a complete success.

The people at the next table ordered very fussily and precisely, with much mutual consulting, and their menus were folded away one by one until the waiter bustled off with news of their choices for the kitchen.

I asked our waiter for Victor's untouched steak to be wrapped so we could take it home. The waiter sneered and ordered a busboy to do it. Anne declined salad, cheese, a sweet, and coffee, and I didn't argue, although I would have liked coffee. The waiter shrugged and deposited the already totalled check on our table, showing that he had expected as much.

Anne paid. I had credit cards and cash, which I offered, but she didn't want to talk about it. The busboy returned with the steak wrapped in foil that had been fashioned sarcastically into the shape of a swan, with the neck forming a sort of handle.

We got up to leave. I said, "What about—" and Anne shushed me so furiously that I felt slapped, humiliated. We left the courtyard. As we turned out of the restaurant entrance, and Anne stalked past the empty spot where the Citroën had been parked, I realized we were taking the bus back. Damn. I had been looking forward to the comfort of a car ride after dinner.

We filed along in uncompanionable silence, which was disturbed now and again by the rush of passing cars. It was even weirder to be traipsing along this road at night. Cars sometimes slowed in an alarming way. I felt eyes appraising us. I was following Anne, as before, and could not decipher those shoulders, that stride. I felt like a child, with my party-favor swan. I thought of Victor, driving alone in his Citroën. I ought to feel something like sympathy for him, but I don't. I try to see him through Anne's eyes, but I can't.

The bus stop was lit by a solitary street lamp. It felt futile to wait there, long after any bus might come along, but Anne assured me that they ran hourly.

"What do you suppose Victor is going to do about dinner?" I finally asked, wanting to say something, not that Victor's alimentary requirements were high on my list of concerns.

"That's his Axminster, don't you think?"

"Do you think the woman recognized you?"

"I don't see how she could have, as she's never seen me."

"Where do you suppose Annamarie thinks Victor is tonight?"

"I haven't the foggiest. I never think about that."

"Don't you think you ought to, from time to time?"

There was the longest, most uncomfortable silence. Like a mirage, our bus came into view.

Oh, Benedict.

Is this what love is, what love makes people do? On the one hand: would you hide under a table for me? On the other hand: why the hell would you need to? Maybe I'm just smug because I've got you, and, compared to this, ours is a simple life. Sometimes, for admittedly brief interludes, I persuade myself that it's all romantic, and European, and I'm a gauche American with naïve ideas about how the world is.

But no. This is awful. I could leave before my two weeks are up, but Anne wants me here; she's made several cryptic remarks about how important this visit is to her. Maybe I'm supposed to bear witness to this glorious erotic connection. Maybe I'm supposed to pass judgment. (Ignatz Mouse *wanted* to go to jail, remember. Am I here to see the flung brick and play Offissa Pup?)

And then there's you, whom I miss very much. How is life at the most uncompetitive tennis camp in New England? I picture you surrounded by rich children in tennis whites scarfing down hot dogs while you sweat over the grill. Luckies. They are sunburned and demanding. You are sunburned and patient. There is red clay staining your sneakers and the left pocket of your shorts. You wish you could have a beer. A camper with a bee sting cries. Smoke gets in your eyes.

If you think I sound confused about Anne and Victor, you're right. I don't know which I fear more: feeling I might have to do something, or feeling I can't do anything. And which would be worse? Do I just want to punish Victor? Could Annamarie possibly be grateful for a note, a telephone call, or would that be a betrayal of Anne, despite its being for the best? And would it be for the best?

I've got to go, but one more thing. When I was seven, I was standing on the corner at Second Avenue and Fifty-ninth Street with my grandmother—we were on our way to Central Park—when a little boy darted into the street in front of us. Gay let go of my hand and lifted him up onto the sidewalk with a quick underarm hoist, and then he turned around in a fury, no little boy at all but a middle-aged dwarf, with acne scars and a Don Ameche mustache. He was about my height.

"Fuck you, lady!" he said—a reasonable response, I suppose, to being rescued when you don't need to be rescued at all. But maybe he was in danger. I've never thought of that possibility until right now. Maybe she did the right thing. What do you think?

I love you for sentimental reasons—

Harriet

Sleeping

SHE WOULD NOT HAVE to change a diaper, they said. In fact, she would not have to do anything at all. Mrs. Winter said that Charles would not wake while she and Mr. Winter were out at the movies. He was a very sound sleeper, she said. No need to have a bottle for him or anything. Before the Winters left they said absolutely please don't look in on the sleeping baby because the door squeaked too loudly.

Harriet had never held a baby, except for one brief moment, when she was about six, when Mrs. Antler next door had surprisingly bestowed on her the tight little bundle that was their new baby, Andrea. Harriet had sat very still and her arms had begun to ache from the tension by the time Mrs. Antler took back her baby. Andy was now a plump seven-year-old, older than Harriet had been when she held her that day.

After two hours of reading all of the boring mail piled neatly on a desk in the bedroom and looking through a depressing wedding album filled with photographs of dressed-up people in desperate need of orthodonture (Harriet had just ended two years in braces and was very conscious of malocclusion issues) while flipping channels on their television, Harriet turned the knob on the baby's door very tentatively, but it seemed locked. She didn't dare turn the knob with more pressure because what if she made a noise and woke him and he started to cry?

She stood outside the door and tried to hear the sound of a baby breathing, but she couldn't hear anything through the

27

door except the sound of the occasional car that passed by on the street outside. She wondered what Charles looked like. She wasn't even sure how old he was. Why had she agreed to babysit when Mr. Winter approached her at the swim club? She had never seen him before, and it was flattering that he took her for being capable, as if just being a girl her age automatically qualified her as a babysitter.

By the time the Winters came home, Harriet had eaten most of the M&Ms in the glass bowl on their coffee table: first all the brown ones, then the orange ones, then all the green ones, and so on, leaving, in the end, only the yellow.

They gave her too much money and didn't ask her about anything. Mrs. Winter seemed to be waiting for her to leave before checking on the baby. Mr. Winter drove her home in silence. When they reached her house he said, My wife. He hesitated, then he said, You understand, don't you? And Harriet answered, Yes, without looking at him or being sure what they were talking about, although she did really know what he was telling her, and then she got out of his car and watched him drive away.

Louisa Huntington's Last Caller,
at Easter

Louisa Huntington applied lipstick to the delicate outer edge of her eyelids, lightly tracing the line in a practiced gesture. Her famous eyelashes had once been a lush emblem of an entire era of charming and amusing people. Her picture on the wall at Sardi's was little more than a few dashes indicating the face that went with those eyelashes. Now, the face was unrecognizable without considerable retouching, and the trademark eyelashes had become wispy and pale.

But something was really wrong. Louisa looked into the mirror and scowled at her reflection. If she didn't put on her eyeglasses, an act she was loath to do, even in the privacy of her bedroom, she wouldn't be able to apply her makeup. Desperate, she snatched up her glasses from the litter on her dressing table, and deployed them a few inches in front of her face, the way she might once have flourished a jeweled lorgnette.

Louisa gasped at the sight of herself. With the glasses in one hand, she aimed them to peer down at the object she held in the other. Lipstick. She turned it over to read the tiny printing at its flat end, as if some face-saving explanation might be found there. *Wet suede.* She dropped the lipstick and reached for a tissue with which to wipe away her mistake before it could be detected by the tiresome Miss Mindin. Miss Mundane. Descended from a long line of spinsters, no doubt.

It was quite difficult, really, to accommodate Miss Bossy Boots Mindin, but there had been no way around it. Louisa's daughter, Madeleine (a dull, sensible woman whose suburban existence with her pleasant husband and three children was a continuous puzzle to Louisa), had made it quite clear that there were worse things than having a companion, really sort of a personal secretary, living with her in the spare room down at the end of the hall.

Madeleine called this a choice she was giving her mother, but Louisa had slowly come to realize that she wasn't being given any choices, not really. Miss Marjorie Mindin or a nursing home. Miss Mindin or bust.

It takes a great deal of time, and effort, to look one's best, but Louisa couldn't imagine looking anything less than impeccable, even on days that held nothing in store beyond a trip to the podiatrist. And today being Easter, with Steven Knox coming to take her out for lunch, Louisa was especially determined to look terrific.

People rarely asked, "Louisa, how do you do it?" anymore, for the simple reason that she no longer did it, she didn't radiate that ageless, clock-cheating vitality for which she had been renowned. These days, Louisa looked like what she was: a remarkably sturdy ninety-three-year-old. Spry. That was the word, a word used only to describe the elderly.

In recent years, Louisa had noticed that she had fewer friends and more acquaintances. Her oldest friends who hadn't actually died might just as well have, they were so decrepit and feeble and joyless. Obsessed with their digestive systems and their estates. And deaf! Louisa had absolutely hated her last lunch with Marion Harper, whom she had known since Miss Waltham's School for Girls. This was just before Miss Mindin. The poor thing couldn't hear a single word Louisa said unless she shouted, there had been trouble when the waiter brought the wrong food and insisted it was what Louisa had ordered, and then Marion had been shirty with her about Steven Knox.

"This young man you're going around with—he is, after all, a bit light in the loafers, isn't he, dear?" Marion had opined over the erroneous omelets. Bitch. She would know. Consider her husband, Otis Harper, dead these twenty years.

"I really don't know what you mean, Marion," Louisa had said with exaggerated, cold clarity, and regretted instantly not having taken the higher conversational road of ignoring the remark entirely.

"Well, I'm sure he's very good company, my dear, but I cannot help but think about poor Lillian Mortimer, that's all." Marion had eyed her triumphantly. She really did look decrepit. And silly, with two bright spots of old-fashioned rouge daubed on her cheeks.

Marion rattled on about Lillian Mortimer and how awful it was that her children and grandchildren hadn't taken more trouble to look after her at the end. Louisa tried not to listen. Throughout her entire life, Louisa had never liked spending time with old people. Why should anyone expect her to start liking it now?

Lillian Mortimer's sad fate had nothing to do with Louisa. Years and years ago, Lillian had been widowed unexpectedly when Edward, who was much older than she, dropped dead on the fourth tee at some Florida resort or other, and then there had been unattractive legal matters for quite a long while because Edward seemed to have left the Mortimer homestead in Northbury, Connecticut, and all his investments not to Lillian and their three grown children, but in trust for the benefit of his secretary, some twenty-three-year-old nothing from outer Queens.

Lillian had died two years ago? Was it five? She was living in a nursing home by then. Louisa hadn't ever gone to see her after the move. There had been a couple of phone calls, but then Lillian had a stroke. Louisa knew that if she were in Lillian's situation, she would never want anyone to see her with half her face drooping down, saliva running out the corner of her mouth, wearing whatever some stupid-as-hell nurse thought to dress her in. It would be simply out of the question.

"I hope you haven't changed your will. It was a terribly difficult and thoughtless thing that Edward did to that family."

"Steven Knox doesn't want my money, Marion. What an offensive thing to say. Really!"

"What is it that Madeleine calls him? Steven Noxious?"

The problem with Marion Harper was that despite her deafness and increasing forgetfulness, she had an uncanny knack for not only eliciting from you various personal tidbits, but also recalling them at moments like this.

"Madeleine is a wet blanket. I really don't understand how my only child could have selected her genes entirely from the Huntington side of the family. The Hodgson sense of style seems to have been swamped by the Huntington stodginess. Maybe one of those over-indulged grandchildren of mine will rebel against her and enjoy life."

That shut Marion up for the moment. Louisa put an end to this annoying discussion by beckoning the waiter for their check. They pretended it was her turn to treat, but it was always her turn to treat, as she had money and Marion really just got by.

Ridiculous personage, the waiter. Who cared if his name was Philip? "I shall call you Waiter, if and when I call you anything," Louisa had interrupted at the first launching of his eager introductory remarks.

"My, my, aren't we getting all dolled up!" Miss Mindin was in the doorway. The door had been closed. Miss Mindin had not knocked. Louisa continued to gaze at her own reflection in the dressing table mirror. Miss Mindin stepped closer until Louisa could see the phony-baloney smile gleaming over her shoulder. Miss Mindin wore starchy white blouses over ghastly stretch pants which she called "slacks." Although it wasn't a uniform, something about her made it look like one. Personal secretary my foot. White blouses, Louisa had informed her right off the bat, reminded Louisa of snow, and virginity, and other useless things.

Madeleine had gone directly to the accountant, Mr. Teeth and Gums, what was his name? Mr. Low. (Suspiciously short name for someone with a nose like that, Louisa thought. Surely his forebears had discarded some syllables at Ellis Island.) She had done this the day after she observed Louisa mistakenly attempt to eat her scrambled eggs with a ballpoint pen instead of a fork—a simple error made when Louisa was tired and of course not wearing her glasses.

Louisa could just imagine Madeleine meeting with him, feeling terribly virtuous and concerned about her scatter-brained mother. They had worked long and hard to procure the Mindin creature from some agency that specialized in supplying "companions." If she wanted companionship, Louisa would have got a dog. A whippet, like Argyle. He had been a grand little fellow, and such good company.

Oh, they had a fine time arranging all the details, spending her money. Madeleine and Mr. T & G worked it all out before they told her the first thing. It was a party to which Louisa had not been invited. A fete accompli, she might once have murmured to appreciative ears at just the right moment at an amusing dinner. It was the classic sort of Louisa Huntington remark that would have been circulated, printed in the society columns.

"I said, aren't we getting all dolled up?" Miss Mindin repeated, now picking up a sweater of Louisa's and putting it in the wrong drawer.

"I really wouldn't say that *we* were anything in particular, if I were you," Louisa said, moving her mouth as little as possible while applying foundation.

"Well, somebody's all wound up today," Miss Mindin observed in her nursey voice. She wouldn't have been able to get "dolled up" if her life depended on it. Miss Mindin was like a cross between a nun and a policewoman.

"*Somebody* had that door shut," Louisa said. Her hand holding the mascara wand trembled slightly. She waited for it to steady before beginning to stroke her lashes with the tiny brush.

"Wound up and touchy, too," said Miss Mindin agreeably, as though she were taking inventory for some checklist. Maybe she was. Did Madeleine get written reports of her mother's sleeping problems, her bowel movements, her moods? Probably. What a thought.

"I am expecting a caller. We are going for an Easter lunch. You are not invited." There. Was that frosty enough?

"Steven Knox isn't supposed to take you anywhere without me, Louisa. You know that. Madeleine explained to me all about what happened the last time he took you out. You went to the bathroom and got confused. Remember?" Miss Mindin was using her reasonable voice.

"I don't see why you need to come. Find your own man. Not that you'd know how." The bathroom business was ridiculous. Louisa hadn't been able to make out the signs on the doors, that was all. The restaurant to which Steven had taken her was dark. Yes, she had a couple of cocktails. Yes, she had noticed the urinal, but Steven often took her to amusing places that had been made over from other sorts of places.

Only when Louisa had been washing her hands, and she was trying to puzzle out the meaning of a sign over the urinal that said WE AIM TO PLEASE, YOU AIM TOO, PLEASE, did it begin to dawn on her that this was not the ladies' room. The man who came in just then, already unzipped, waterworks at hand, was most unpleasant. There was no need to make such a scene. Were he not so rude, Louisa would not have sneered, "You call *that* a penis?" Had she refrained from the remark, the man would probably not have reported her to the manager, and she and Steven would not have been asked to leave.

But it was a simple mistake, going in there, not a sign of senility. It had happened to Louisa before, years ago, at a hunt club dance in Newport where the bathroom doors were labeled POINTERS and SETTERS, for God's sake. The real mistake had been in telling Madeleine the story, which was, after all, rather amusing.

Louisa was finished with her face. She stood and turned. "I am going to get dressed now, in the privacy of my own room."

Miss Mindin smirked, and ostentatiously backed out of the room in a parody of respect. Louisa closed the door and then stood against it, listening. As she suspected, Miss Mindin was telephoning. She could hear the pinchy sound of the Mindin voice without being able to make out the words. Oh well. Madeleine would be proposing some tiresome compromise, perhaps something along the lines of Miss Mindin sitting alone at the next table, as though she and Steven were independent little children being supervised in public.

In her slip, Louisa spritzed herself with Joy. What to wear? Louisa thought the Balenciaga suit. Hard to believe it was sixty years old. She had bought it in Milan, on an anniversary trip with Arthur. He had liked the way she looked in it, and he had told her she ought to wear pink more often. She could still remember the afternoon she bought the suit, the flirtatious tailor who fitted it. So many things change, but a good Balenciaga suit is forever. The suit was twice as old as Steven Knox.

He would be here very soon. Thirty-four isn't all that young. By the time Louisa was thirty-four, Madeleine was eleven, Arthur was already involved with that Contessa (no one thought it would last, but it did), and Louisa was already feeling her age when she surveyed the competition.

Steven Knox was an unusual young man. No one in his generation was particularly informed about Louisa's era. But he knew everything, and he was deeply interested. It wasn't just trivia to him. He could sing all the words to songs she had forgotten. He could name people and events Louisa hadn't thought about in years, people and events no one else talked about anymore.

Though every now and then someone did write up a nostalgia piece, on the anniversary or revival of something or other, and if an editor was old enough to know about Louisa Huntington, some little reporter would arrive, obviously astonished to find her sentient, and attempt to interview her.

"You must have had such an interesting life," squeaked the last one, a girl with nice enough features but no sense at all about how to dress or the value of a good hairstyle, let alone knowledge of depilatories.

"I'm still having it," Louisa replied, dry as could be, though the point of such remarks was now entirely her own amusement.

This was why Steven Knox was such a relief. He loved her wit. He already knew most of her best lines before they met. They had met . . . well, Louisa didn't really like to say how they met. It was a pickup, more or less, at the glove counter at Saks. Where he worked. Where he used to work. Oh, what did it matter? What Madeleine didn't know wouldn't hurt her.

Miss Mindin was off the phone, her strategy in place, and was now in the hall bathroom. Louisa eased her door open partway and listened to the sound of water running. Miss Mindin probably washed according to some instruction chart: First scrub body part A. Rinse thoroughly.

Louisa stood outside the bathroom door. The key was in the lock. Careless, careless. Miss Mindin didn't want the key left in the lock on the inside of the bathroom door, because *someone* might accidentally lock herself in. It had happened.

Louisa turned the key to lock the door. Scrub those Mindin body parts well. Take all the time you want.

The doorman buzzed from downstairs. Louisa removed the key and walked briskly toward the foyer. She put the key down in the bowl on the front-hall table, where, under the Mindin Regime, all keys must be kept. Pre-Mindin, Louisa had locked herself out many times. That's what the nice man with the Dalmatian across the hall was there for. It had never been a big problem, save the last occasion, when the Dalmatian man was away, which became one of the mouth-pursing "episodes" Madeleine had invoked when making the case for Miss Mindin.

"Send him up!" Louisa shouted into the speaker thing on the wall. She was never certain when she was supposed to push which button. A loud banging began in the hall bathroom.

"Don't be naughty, Louisa. How dare you lock me in here. You open the door right now!" Miss Mindin called. She was silent a moment. "Louisa? Are you there? Are you all right? Don't be angry with me, lovey." Miss Mindin was covering all the bases, alternating between a scolding and a wheedling tone. She began to pound on the door again.

Out in the hallway, the elevator door opened and closed. Louisa knew its noise. She could still recall the sound the old elevator door made, with the sliding metal gate. The building had been modernized a long time ago. Twenty years? Thirty? Harry, the day man, used to run to the liquor store for her.

The doorbell chimed. Louisa checked herself in the mirror. The suit was really excellent, the color just right for an Easter lunch. She grimaced into her reflection, baring her teeth and peering at an angle. Lipstick on teeth should get the death penalty. But not to worry. However, one must remember to stand up straight. Dowager's humps are for dowagers. Louisa threw back her shoulders, picked up her small alligator clutch, and opened the door.

Steven Knox was standing there, looking handsome as always. He was wearing a very large yellow bow tie that went perfectly with his striped shirt and tweed jacket. His hair was parted in the middle in the old-fashioned way, and just now he tossed his head back to flip a few strands out of his eyes, a gesture that always made Louisa think of restless race horses. He was holding a bouquet of sweetheart roses.

Before he could say more than the usual "Lu!" (to which she would always reply with a coy and girlish "*Tu!*"), she plucked the roses from him and tossed them behind her into the foyer, stepping out into the hall and pulling the door shut in one graceful, charming gesture.

"I'm all set, my darling. Shall we?" She pushed the elevator button impatiently and the doors slid open. Steven kissed her on the cheek as she took his arm and they stepped into the elevator.

"You're looking lovely," he said, appraising her. "The Balenciaga from Milan? And joy of joys, you're Mindin-less!" The pounding sound could be heard faintly as they began to descend. Steven tilted his head inquisitively.

"Someone must be hanging a picture," said Louisa, who was drawing on her pale gray gloves. "It's so easy to crack plaster if you don't do it just right."

Out on the sidewalk in front of her building it was extraordinarily bright, and the air had a soft, sun-warmed feeling. One could do so many things on a day like this. Two black women in white uniforms passed, talking in animated voices in a language or dialect Louisa didn't know. Perhaps they were from the same island. They walked slowly, pushing matching white babies in fancy strollers.

The nannies glanced simultaneously at Louisa, and then both smiled as they glided past. Such beautiful white teeth. One said something to the other, and the liquid, silvery trills of their laughter floated behind them, wafted by the breeze of a passing taxi.

The Dalmatian man nodded hello. Louisa nodded back. He was carrying a little plastic bag, for the dog mess, and he was wearing shorts, which wasn't really a good idea for those legs. The Dalmatian dawdled behind him, hoisting a leg high over the bed of ivy by the curb.

A young couple suddenly flew by on those new roller skates with wheels that look like blades. They wore tight black outfits, and they held hands as they darted together through traffic. The way they moved reminded Louisa of dancing.

I still want all this, Louisa thought. I'm not ready to give up my life. I simply won't allow them to take what's mine.

The doorman—the little one, whose name was José or Juan or something like that, Louisa couldn't keep track anymore, not since Mike retired—asked if they needed a taxi. In the old days, doormen were much, much taller, and they called one Mrs. Huntington, not sweetheart.

"No, I wouldn't dream of it, thank you just the same," Louisa said, with a wave of her gloved hand. She slipped the other one through Steven Knox's proffered arm. "It's glorious weather, and we've got the whole afternoon."

Shooting in Sequence

"THE CASTLETOWNHAVEN BRIDGE has but the one lane, and drivers must go one at a time from either end anyway, so making them wait a few more minutes during a take won't be too hard to manage at all."

A *take*. David Cooper smiled through his impatience and wondered if Donal Hurley had the least idea of the meaning of half the lingo he had picked up during the shoot—*the shoot*—on location with the American film crew of "Rock of the Cats." Donal's location reports to David, the film's director, were always larded with advice.

"Local lads with walkie-talkies stationed on each side to control the traffic whilst you're shooting for the five days would be a few quid well spent," Donal added.

Now that they had completed two weeks of shooting on Sherkin Island, filming of the next segment was to begin in Castletownhaven in the morning. The story, an IRA romance set in the 1920's, was being shot in sequence. "Rock of the Cats" was a low-budget, no-name production, and the mood on the set was primarily one of boredom—no one in the cast or crew harbored the illusion that he was achieving a career pinnacle. David Cooper had been a name once, a rising star, but somehow none of his films had ever quite lived up to expectations.

In his twenties he was experimental, a wunderkind. In his thirties he had gotten bad breaks, some deals had gone sour, some stars had pulled out of films, and while a couple of his movies had matched his earlier critical success, they were all box office duds. In his forties there had been a well-publicized affair with the married star of his mega-disaster nightmare film that one critic characterized famously as like "Ishtar," only without the artistic integrity. This had been followed by a well-publicized divorce, some well-publicized drinking problems, and, finally, a well-publicized stint at Betty Ford.

Now, at fifty-two, after some humiliatingly menial television work (second location director, technical stuff with no responsibilities attached), David Cooper had been gone so long (five years being like forever) that he had become obscure, a name barely recognized by the younger executives at the studios. He had been given "Rock of the Cats" by a twenty-two-year-old kid at Dreamcastle, Benjamin Sears, a smart-aleck from Connecticut who seemed to have unlimited power. Benjamin signed him to direct the picture because, he said, he had a lot of respect for David Cooper, having been profoundly influenced by David's first feature, which he happened to see on television when he was fourteen.

The construction crew had been in the village for a week ahead of the film crew, and were nearly finished with their anachronistic improvements to the shopfronts along the main street of the village. Castletownhaven had a new authentic period veneer of grimness concealing all the modern touches of color that gratified the tourists in recent times.

Now it was the end of the afternoon of the first day in Castletownhaven, the sound mix people seemed to be plagued by equipment problems, and various members of the crew were urgently wanting David's attention. But he was having the meeting with Donal and the Assistant Production Manager, Jane Barnes, a businesslike woman in her forties, half-Brit, half-Irish, with whom David seemed to have begun something two nights before in his room over the pub on Sherkin.

Probably a mistake, nothing more than an unwise indiscretion. It had a been a long time. He couldn't sort it out right now.

Locals, according to Jane, seemed eager to cooperate with the production. The film was spreading money around the village—every B&B was filled, the pubs were doing a roaring trade—and besides, everyone was excited, there was a movie being made right under their noses. David should be able to capitalize on that for cooperation, on the feeling that Hollywood was on the doorstep here in County Cork, that fame and glory and tourists would be coming to Castletownhaven, never mind the movie had no famous star from America. Closing the bridge, however, might be a P.R. problem, as it would inconvenience the tourists, which could hurt business.

"The Germans, aye," agreed Donal with a sour nod. A retired joiner from Skibbereen whose nephew Colin was both a union official and an electrician on the set, Donal's official title was Location Manager, but his employment was actually for the dual purpose of supervising construction and acting as a diplomatic go-between with the locals.

"Germans are the worst, they are. Always in a rush. Oh, they are. Wanting everything the way they want it. Immediately if not at once. Germans. The worst."

"Look, you'll just have to deal with it," said David, checking his watch impatiently. "Hire the lads. Good idea." He had a lot to do before they shut down for the night. They were already on overtime; soon enough they'd be into waltz time. Every meeting with Donal seemed to take an hour. Did the man understand anything about the time factor in making films? And he repeated himself endlessly. David had discovered during those first days of filming on Sherkin that if he wasn't listening when Donal said something, it would come around again, and again. And even if no one at all was listening, even if people had begun to walk away, Donal would talk until he was finished. David would have to see if Jane had any strategies for limiting meetings with Donal.

"The French are just as bad, drive all over the road, they do, oh they do. All over the road. Not a signal. No, all over the road they are. Worthless crowd."

David rolled his eyes at Jane, who grimaced back at him helplessly. Donal supposed these two thought he was simple, that he didn't know about their carry-on.

He ignored them and concluded, "Aye, 'tis the Germans and the French who'll be making the trouble for us if the bridge is closed when one of them needs to be getting someplace, see if they don't. Oh, see if they don't. 'Tis trouble they'll make. The Germans and the French."

It was the third day of the Castletownhaven shoot, and the production was still on schedule. Because they were shooting in sequence, David wanted to feel secure about having enough material in the can, and he was overshooting a bit, but there had been no serious delays from scene to scene. Miraculously, it hadn't even rained significantly. But the catering tent, located in a farmer's field just outside the town, had somehow served lunch to slightly more than twice the number of cast and crew. Jane was informed of this by Marty the accountant, who testily told her to figure it out and report back.

Jane was annoyed with the assignment. Marty had no idea how disliked he was by just about everyone in the crew. And the locals took a scunner to him the first night in the pub on Sherkin, when he told a joke about the Irish farmer who won the Nobel Prize—because he was out standing in his field, Marty had explained to his silent audience, not once but twice.

But David felt obligated to importune Jane to station herself outside the catering tent where she could watch the line form the next day. So here she was. Cast and extras, all dressed in period costume—Jane had told David it all looked to her like primordial Ralph Lauren—were punctuated by the occasional blood-spattered ambush victim risen from the carnage of the morning's scenes. Most of the grips and gaffers seemed to be wearing woolly new Irish sweaters that made them look as if they were about to perform in a soap commercial.

The problem was soon apparent. Local people from the village were drifting into the queue with admirable finesse. Jane could identify them by the flashes of brightly-colored, American-style sportswear peeping out from under the filthy waxed shooting jackets and the like which they had donned for camouflage. Well. There were only two more days of shooting in the village and Jane thought it should be ignored. The studio could afford to feed a few more people. But she dreaded the discussion with Marty.

She would have to talk to David about it. Though talking to David had become awkward enough. They hadn't spent any time alone together since the move to Castletownhaven. Jane thought back to the Sherkin night and closed her eyes for a moment. She had no regrets, but maybe he had a few. Or wasn't there still a wife in the picture? No, he had said he was divorced, and he didn't seem like a liar. David Cooper was intriguing, but ultimately he might be too tired, too American.

After lunch that day the crew began to gear up for the big crowd scene in the Square, the principal reason Castletownhaven had been chosen for a location. Extras eddied around the jarvey cart that lay on its side. The drugged donkey was sprawled in its traces, snoring, lying in the road as if shot. Fake blood was being painted onto his belly while the veterinarian from the village crouched over the donkey, pulling up one eyelid to confirm that Mrs. Mehigan's Old Jack was out cold.

The vet gave a thumbs up, and David's assistant held up three fingers to David, signaling near-readiness. Standing in the doorway of the production trailer, David held up five fingers in return, hoping he could wind up the so-called budget meeting with Marty. The assistant nodded and began to shoo the extras into approximate positions.

David turned back and peered into the dim trailer interior where Marty sat at the little table, receipts piled high, jabbing at columns of figures with his pencil, his calculator clicking away unpleasantly.

"They're not going to like these daily numbers on the Coast, I know that for sure," Marty said. "And I don't like them, either. I know you're overshooting. I'm not as dumb as I look, you know."

"Are you sure, Marty, that it's appropriate to call LA 'the Coast' when you're on the west coast of Ireland?" David had always been openly hostile with number-crunchers like Marty, but in the past days he had begun to appreciate the gently ironic tones he was hearing every evening in the pub. Jane talked that way, too. Must be her Irish side. He would have to find a moment to talk to Jane.

Marty underlined some numbers furiously, for emphasis. In the close atmosphere of the trailer he had broken a sweat under his heavy new fisherman's knit sweater. The sleeves were pushed up his arms, and bunched absurdly, like prosthetic biceps.

"Look, Marty, kiddo, I'm not trying to brush you off, but I don't want to lose the light. Then we'd have to re-shoot tomorrow. I don't have to tell you what that would cost. Look, I have no idea why we fed almost two hundred people today. There are about forty crew, about ten principal cast, about twenty extras. That's it. Did you have lunch today? Okay, that's one more. And there's the farmer whose field we're using. He gets lunch. But we shouldn't exceed a hundred even if we're feeding the traffic boys as well."

"We're feeding half the village, is all I know," said Marty. "I asked Jane to keep an eye. Talk to her. Okay? I'm sure she can explain it. Just don't nickel and dime me to death."

David was impatient to get the shot before the donkey woke

up and crapped or most of the extras had to go home and milk their cows. He signaled out the doorway to his assistant that he needed one more minute. "Anything else?"

"Yeah. Okay. I'll handle it just fine," Marty said, not looking up from his calculations. "Here's how. There will be sign-in sheets in the catering tent from now on, which should be enough rain to cancel that parade. But there's one other item for this week I absolutely don't get. What in hell are you doing with 'three truckloads of hot tarmacadam at a cost of one hundred pounds per load' for the love of Christ?"

David was half out the door of the trailer, and he stopped on the step and turned back to Marty.

"It was because we closed the bridge yesterday afternoon every time we were shooting. It was our last day of shooting on the bridge. Apparently, traffic was backed up pretty badly. There was a load of hot paving material cooling on a truck, and the guy was hopping, threatening to lean on his horn and ruin the shot, said he was going to have to pay for it himself if it didn't get delivered on time, said he didn't give a monkey's toss about wrecking the shot, and he was revving his motor, which we were picking up so we couldn't shoot anyway, so I authorized Fred to tell him we'd give him the price of the load, no hard feelings, if he turned off his motor."

"That's *one* truckload of hot tarmacadam."

"Yeah, I know." David turned and jumped down the trailer steps and stood in the high grass for a moment, looking up at the cloud-strewn sky. The air was rinsed and clear, and the field seemed to float in the afternoon light. The absurdity of the transaction he was describing suddenly struck David as the most wonderful instance of everything about this country that he would never be able to articulate in "Rock of the Cats." The film would probably never even reach theaters in the States—it would go straight to video and in a few years would be considered a minor achievement, a curiosity, a faulty film from a somewhat talented director known for faulty films.

"The thing was, Marty, it was only the middle of the afternoon. Two more loaded trucks showed up needing to cross the bridge before we were done, the drivers demanding to know where were the daft fillum people who were paying top price for hot tarmacadam. So call it luck that the first guy didn't come along any earlier in the day."

Without bothering to wait for a response from Marty, David began to move away from the trailer door, out across the field and into the golden afternoon where everyone was waiting for him. He could see Donal standing under a tree, his pipe in his mouth. Jane, standing beside him, saluted David with a wave of her clipboard that made him feel a tiny flutter of, well, something. Who knows, maybe he needed more of Jane, not less.

"Places!" shouted an assistant. The veterinarian scrambled to his feet beside the donkey and moved out of range.

"It was luck," said David as he headed toward the cameras. It occurred to him that he was talking to himself just like Donal, as Marty couldn't possibly still hear him. It also occurred to him that he was happier at this moment than he could remember having been in years.

"So think of it that way," David murmured. Some of the camera people were sending each other raised-eyebrow looks. David paused to peer through the camera eyepiece before settling into his chair.

"Quiet on the set!" shouted the assistant, poised with the clapper board in front of the camera.

As the buzz of conversation died away, David could be heard concluding, "Pure luck, really, that the truck came along as late in the day as it did. Pure luck. That's what it was. I don't know what else you could call it. Otherwise, by now we'd be the biggest investors in hot tarmacadam this island's ever seen. Pure luck."

Party Animals Like It's 1982

Business at Away in a Manger was not good for a Saturday, consisting as it did only of Bric and Brac, the pair of elderly apricot toy poodles with psoriasis; Happy, a demented Old English Sheepdog with the worst pit knots Lydia had ever seen; and Heinz, the incontinent longhaired dachshund whose owner, a retired piano teacher with time on her hands, brought him for a bath several times a month because of the frequency with which he "widdled himself."

The alarming ring of the annoying new telephone drilled through the Mozart concerto Lydia was listening to while working on this morning's challenging customer. It seemed to relax most dogs, and Mozart reminded her of childhood piano recitals. When she was seven, she had won a prize for her slow but accurate performance of "Away With Melancholy." The sharp shrill of the phone was startling, and she accidentally jerked the de-matting comb with which she was operating on Happy the matted mess, who was bound and trussed on the grooming table. He shivered and rolled his eyes. Tripod, the three-legged shop cat who liked to doze on the counter, woke up and hopped across the counter indignantly.

"I got it!" yelled Corky, Lydia's assistant, from the tub room where she was giving the poodles their medicated bath.

"Don't leave those dogs! They're little shits! They're escape artists!" Lydia yelled back. Lucrative poodles with back injuries she didn't need.

"Waynamaneja, kin I *hep* you?" Corky chirped into the phone, just beating the answering machine. She stood on tippy-toes, stretching dramatically to keep one poodle-policing hand in the air by the tub while holding the telephone receiver with the other. Twenty, unreasonably pretty, Corky was always posing as if for some old-fashioned girlie calendar, flashing that perfectly tanned midriff, Lydia thought, enviously. A New England winter would surely modify her outfits. Lydia semaphored through the tub room doorway, signaling to Corky with a writing gesture to take a message.

After two months of working for Lydia, Corky had developed immunity to any hints that she might consider answering the telephone in a less incomprehensible way. Lydia had begun to hate the sound of her own *I may be a penurious and unhappy divorcee, but I'm in charge of this failing business, damn it* voice insisting relentlessly (and fruitlessly) that Corky should slow it down and e-nun-ci-ate to pronounce the absurd name of this dog grooming establishment with extra precision and clarity. Lydia had gone so far as to suggest that Corky should deliberately dial the multiplex cinema in Orange just to hear the long descriptions of each movie in order to pick up some diction tips. Was it really asking too much of Corky to make an effort to say *help* the way people in Connecticut say it?

"Yessuh, Mnnn. You betcha. Okey-dokey. We shorely wee-yull. You too, honey. Buh-*baye*."

Listening to these south of the Mason-Dixon line syllables, Lydia scolded herself. She should just accept the whole Corky package. What was Corky short for? Corky-Sue? Corky-Ann? Corky-Beth? Corky McDougal had traveled "up nawth" under vague and mysterious circumstances, something about her great-aunt who lived in a trailer park in Naugatuck needing companionship after a hip operation. Possibly also something about needing a fresh start.

Lydia's dog grooming establishment, located in Cheshire near the high school, had only been open for a few months when Corky floated into the shop one slow afternoon to buy a flea collar for her aunt's cat. Tripod the marmalade tabby was sunning himself in the front window. As she bent to pet him, his missing leg startled Corky, and her eyes had overflowed with tears. Lydia explained that she had rescued the poor cat from the clutches of a cut-rate veterinarian in Prospect—according to the UPS guy, he was addicted to horse tranquilizers—who was going to euthanize him, having misunderstood a Portuguese factory worker's gestured request to trim the cat's nails. This made Corky outright sob.

Lydia was touched by Corky's genuine sympathy for Tripod, a welcome antidote to the reserve and decorum of Connecticut. After an hour of chatter about cats and dogs, the grooming business, and the admittedly perplexing name of the shop, Corky had walked out of Away in a Manger with the feline flea collar and a part-time job. Lydia's impulsive offer had surprised them both. So far it had worked out; Corky's implicit hayseed qualities made people assume she had some sort of an agricultural background which made them trust her with their pets. And Lydia appreciated what a hard worker she was, and good company, too, though her perkiness was hard to take some mornings.

Lydia turned back to Happy and scissored out the last knot from the tender inside of his left hindquarter. The pink skin there, naked now except for some wispy white hairs, was somehow touching and as private as the inadvertently exposed parts of dignified elderly people. She ruffled his head.

"Good boy, that's a good doggie. Three pits down, one to go." Happy sighed and dropped his head back onto the steel table. Lydia wondered sometimes what he thought about while she was grooming him. He was sixteen. His owners, the Gillespies, a couple of tweedy academics now retired from the English department at the community college in Hamden, apparently didn't understand that an occasional gentle pass with a wire brush would save everybody concerned a certain amount of anguish.

Happy's days were definitely numbered. He had become so forgetful that he no longer remembered when he had to pee, even after he had barked to go out. He would head out onto the grass, stand there a moment, and then return to the kitchen door and yip to be admitted, Mr. and Mrs. Gillespie told Lydia in anxious confiding tones as though she were their child's therapist, only to relieve himself moments later in the privacy of the space under the dining room table. Arthur Gillespie was also convinced that Happy didn't recognize him a lot of the time.

"He's faking, I can tell," Arthur insisted. "He's just being polite. My uncle Richard was the same when he came down with Alzheimer's. Thought I was my late father, then his father, then at the end he didn't even have a clue we had ever met and would introduce himself. He urinated in the umbrella stand by the front door the last time he came to our house. It was terribly embarrassing."

Lydia raised her voice and called into the back, "Cork? Who was that on the phone?"

"That guy."

"What guy?"

"The consultant guy. You know. He's comin' at noon."

"Somebody's bringing his dog at noon? It's Saturday—we close at noon."

"No, no, you remember, Lydia hon. The *consultant guy.* He's comin' to *consult.*"

"Did I make this appointment, Corky? Is he trying to sell us something? We don't need anything. There isn't anything I can afford."

"I *tole* ya, Sweetcakes, he's gonna *consult* with us. I had the phone call with him that day last week? You were on the road with that Schnauzer you delivered to Northbury? For the

Levines? And I tole him he could come on in, but I tole you about and you said it was okey-dokey."

Sweetcakes. Okey-dokey. *Oy vey iz mir*, as Corky's antecedents never used to say.

"I did?"

"Yes, ma'am, you did."

"Don't ma'am me!"

"You betcha."

Harold Blinder—the consultant guy—was punctual. Saturdays were half-days, and all the dogs had been picked up by eleven-thirty. At five of twelve, from where she perched at the front counter by the bin of rawhide dog chews, doing triage on some bills and spooning down the remains of a dubious yogurt from the fridge while Corky vacuumed, Lydia could see him sitting out front in his parked car. He seemed to be studying her shop sign.

She was defensive about the sign, having painted it herself. Away in a Manger was admittedly a misleading name for a grooming parlor that didn't offer animals a place to lay down their sweet heads, evidenced by the boarding inquiries, but you could say that the sign itself was distinctive. Though Lydia did realize in her heart of hearts that letters formed out of cartoon-y dog bones were just never going to be everybody's cup of tea.

At the dot of noon, Harold Blinder applied breath drops vigorously and climbed out of his car clutching a dented aluminum attaché case like the futuristic rocket ship toys of Lydia's childhood. He approached the door to the shop and peered through the glass. Lydia shouted out, "Your guy is here!" to Corky, but Corky couldn't hear her over the roar of the wet vac as she scrubbed at the corners of the tub room.

Harold Blinder, Marketing Consultant, stood just inside the door for a moment, his eyes adjusting to the dim shop interior after noonday sunlight. It took him a moment to locate Lydia. When he did, he went into gear, shouting over the vacuuming din.

"You Lydia Harris? Harold Blinder—that's Blinder rhymes with kindergarten, not Blinder as in watch winder." He approached the counter, stopped, dropped his briefcase into the slot between his feet, and extended his hand with what seemed like the intention of a handshake but was in fact the offer of a card to Lydia. Both his introductory remarks and the business with the card seemed rehearsed.

Lydia had taken off her glasses when she started to fog up while applying cream rinse to Heinz, and she had left them on the counter in the grooming room. She held the business card at arm's length and squinted to read it. She could just bring the words into focus. At forty-six, Lydia had few vanities, but she didn't like the way glasses made her look like a substitute teacher. One thing you could say for the dog bone letters on her sign, they were much easier to read than the discreet, sans-serif typography of Harold Blinder, Marketing Consultant.

Corky stopped vacuuming and was now crashing around at the back door with the rubbish. It always seemed to Lydia that the noise of the vacuum cleaner temporarily drowned out the wet dog smell, when in fact the hot exhaust from the motor enhanced it. A rich blend of flaking poodle, vintage sheepdog, and incontinent dachshund now wafted moistly through the sudden stillness of the small shop.

"Tell me in a sentence why you think I need a marketing consultant?" Lydia said, scritching the top of Tripod's skull. The cat got up, turned around, and re-sprawled luxuriantly on the counter while chirping his appreciation.

"Well Lydia—may I call you Lydia? Please call me Hal—"

"Is that Hal as in salivate or Hal as in calculate?"

"Uh, either one is okay by me. Lydia. As I was saying. You have a real nice business here." He grimaced at Tripod and looked around with unconvincing enthusiasm at the cheap plywood paneling, pausing to take in the bulletin board plastered with snapshots of lost or unwanted cats and dogs. Some days it seemed that half the people who opened the door at Away in a Manger were either desperately searching for a beloved animal or were equally desperate to palm off an undesirable one. Lydia kept a jar marked "donations" for the use of her bulletin board, and no one had ever questioned where the money went. Implicitly, this benefited indigent puppies and kitties; actually, it went toward coffee and donuts.

"I was telling your partner, Corky is it? I was telling Corky on the phone the other day that I think I can help you folks find some new niches in the market."

"Corky is my employee." Lydia said flatly. Where was she? "Corky! Your consultant friend is here!" Lydia shouted into the back.

Corky emerged then. She had applied fresh makeup and re-tied her perfect blonde mane in an adorable French-looking loose braid. Somehow her range was no-effort beautiful to slight-effort knockout beautiful. Lydia watched Hal's expression change.

"Corky? May I call you Corky?" he began eagerly, fumbling madly in a jacket pocket for another card, obviously regretting his false start with Lydia. "Is that short for Corinne?"

Lydia interjected, "Corky, this is Hal Blinder as in hinder. Hal—this is Corky as in—"

"Pleastameetcha," Corky said, proffering a limp hand in his direction, which he grabbed and shook enthusiastically, leaving his card in her palm. She looked at her hand with disappointment at his efficiency. She thought people should take their time with, well, with just about everything.

"Corky—I see a problem here. Major image problem here. Do you know your problem begins before customers even step inside your door?" Hal changed gears suddenly, all dramatic business pitch now.

"Howzat?" Corky looked puzzled.

"Manger. Bad word. Know why? Makes me think: mange. It's why I called you. Don't do many cold calls. People call *me*. Know Harold Blinder's work. When they need me, they call me. But I drive past here a few times a month to see a new client out on Route Five. You must know Freddie's Flapjacks, over near Price Club? 'We flip for you, you'll flip for us'? Every time I pass by and see your sign I think of mange. That's not good. That's bad. Trust me on this. It's *real* bad for a business like yours."

"Wait—" Lydia interrupted. "What happened to Polly's Pancake Parlor?" Lydia had only been there once, with her lawyer, actually, the day her divorce was finalized last year. They had gone directly there from the courthouse, and she had cried silently into her lingonberry crepes. Solicitous Ben Whitney (he of the premature baldness, bow-tie, and red suspenders school of lawyering) had offered her his handkerchief to supplement her shredded paper napkin. Lydia had stuffed the handkerchief into her pocketbook after she stopped crying. It had lingonberry stains.

She had meant to wash it and return it to him right away, but she never did. Its discreet BCW monogram reproached her when she came across the folded linen square in her underwear drawer. Just before she had started to cry that day, it seemed to Lydia that Ben had, perhaps, possibly been on the verge of asking her out to dinner, but the moment went away, if it was a moment, and she hadn't heard from him since, other than a smiley face scribbled next to his signature on the very reasonable bill for his services.

"Polly's Pancake Parlor? 'Do drop in or we'll both starve'? " Hal quoted derisively. "Seriously? Gone. Re-concepted. People eat more pancakes when you call them flapjacks and put a man's name on them. Men do, especially. You know how many men never set foot in the place because it was a 'parlor'? I can tell you. We have numbers on that. 'Parlor' makes people think of two things, both of them bad for business.

Know what those two things are? Funeral. Massage. Can't sell a whole lot of pancakes either way."

Corky was mesmerized. Lydia, too, was fascinated by what he was saying, but the way this Harold Blinder talked! Some of his sentences didn't have subjects.

"Now they get a ton of breakfast meeting business because of the guy thing, the menfolk around the campfire stoking up on victuals thing," Hal continued. (He pronounced that word vick-shu-als and Lydia didn't correct him.) "Got wait staff in there with plaid flannel and ten-gallon hats, got cactus in big pots, got table settings with tin plates and coffee cups. The menu items are called Provisions."

"*You* thought of that slogan? *You* invented 'We flip for you, you'll flip for us'?" Corky was saucer-eyed with awe.

"None other," Hal affirmed modestly.

"I am *so* impressed." Corky turned to Lydia (who was also impressed, but in a different way) for approval. "Lydia, honey, isn't this great? We got us a real expert."

"Why Freddie? Why not Frank's Flapjacks?" Lydia persisted. Something about Harold Blinder made her want to argue with him. Unlike Corky, she had zero feelings of awe.

"Well, Lydia, that's a good question. Very reasonable question. Can you tell that you're the kind of gal who thinks things through. *Like* a gal who does that. Got a good answer to your question."

Hal's tone seemed vaguely condescending, though Lydia couldn't say why. Maybe it was the patronizing tone of "gal." He had stopped talking and was waiting for some cue from her, like someone doing a parlor trick in front of a skeptical audience. She nodded and gestured impatiently that he should go on.

"Studies showed that the name Frank makes people think of hot dogs," Hal revealed triumphantly, as if describing a major scientific breakthrough. Marketing people. "See the problem? Of course you do. Freddie, on the other hand, is both food-neutral and sounds honest, sincere—but not too formal," he added, clearly quoting some insane demographic study from memory. What did they do, have focus groups free-associate about men's names? Probably.

"Well, Freddie's not food-neutral to me," Lydia countered a little belligerently. "I knew a boy named Freddie in high school who picked his nose all through history class. Now he works at the Texaco station out on Route 10. I think Freddie sounds like the name of an automobile mechanic with hairy wrists whose hygiene might be very questionable."

"Hon—" began Corky.

"I'm not done," Lydia interrupted. "I just want to say that my father's name was Frank, and the name doesn't make me think of hot dogs at all. It makes me think of knowing all the names of the constellations. It makes me think of the smell of cigar smoke and coffee beans. He was a coffee wholesaler. There were always scratchy burlap sacks in his back seat. And he made great pancakes, as a matter of fact."

"Lydia, honey! No one's insulting your daddy's memory! This fella is a business expert! Let's listen to his advice, okay?" Corky implored.

"Ladies, shall we cut to the chase?" Hal suggested in a somewhat aggrieved tone.

"Whatever," Lydia said, folding her arms across her chest. What chase? A movie-editing instruction. Get on with the action. Cut to the chase scene. Fine. Corky shot her another beseeching look.

"Cats," Hal said. There was silence.

"What do you mean, cats?" Lydia finally asked. She stroked Tripod defensively.

"Statistically, we're heading toward a day when households will have more cats and fewer dogs. It's inevitable. Everybody working, Granny in Florida, no time for all the walks. Dogs are high maintenance. Cats are low maintenance. Your future lies in providing services for cats."

"But cats don't *need* services, honey, that's why people like 'em. They're what you said? Low maintenance?" Corky broke in. "And they never need grooming! They wash they own little selves all day long with those scratchy tongues they got. The only cats I know need any grooming from us are those lazy, long-haired jobbies, you know, the ones with the pushed-in faces, whattayacallems? Persians. They get full of knots, and they can be mean. We get some of those—strictly sedate and strip."

"You must create the demand," Hal uttered oracularly.

"What do you mean exactly?" Lydia asked, her curiosity piqued. She looked at Tripod again, who stared back at her.

"Look around you." Obediently, Lydia and Corky swiveled around the shop. "No, no, no, no. I don't mean that literally," Hal said crossly. "Look around in the world. Think big, outside this shop. What do you see in the magazines, what do you see when you look at the kids at the mall? The nose rings and bizarre hairdos. The tattoos. With those weirdly shaved heads, and tufts of long hair, they get themselves up like poodles, am I right?" Hal seemed genuinely excited now. He gestured with a pointed finger at the world outside their door for emphasis.

"Now, consider a cat." They both looked down at Tripod. "Look at this cat here. No, don't look at this cat. Or do, fine, but forget the leg thing for a moment. Cats are untouched by human hands, unchanged by trends. Classic. Elegant. Maintenance-free. Am I right or am I right?"

"You're right!" Corky answered, rapt.

"What can we do to change that? What is our strategy? What is our relationship to that?" he asked. Lydia wondered if Hal was winging it now or was he following some New Agey marketing script.

"Think show poodle. Think topiary bushes. Think those mall kids." Hal paused for dramatic emphasis. "It's the last frontier. See it. Know it. Do it."

"What are you saying, exactly?" Lydia persisted, not yet quite clear on his point.

"You are the sculptor. Let cats—and perhaps certain dogs—be your clay."

Lydia and Corky labored for a week in preparation for the grand opening of Party Animals. The shop was closed. The shades were drawn over the window and door, and there was a small sign taped to the glass apologizing for inconvenience and explaining that Away in a Manger would be re-opening tomorrow with a new concept. Not that very many people would see a sign on their door down at this end of the block, the end of the commercial zone on this stretch of South Main Street. No wonder the empty store had been available so cheaply.

Lydia had foraged at the local animal shelter for two litters adding up to eight black kittens, and they cavorted in a playpen, each one sporting a different shaved pattern of stripes, bands or swirling polka dots of eerily bare gray skin. Tumbled together they were living paisley.

Other cats had been rounded up with a series of calls to some of the numbers displayed on the "Looking for a Home" half of the bulletin board. Sulking together in a basket (and emitting a constant sour chorus) were three matching Siamese with total body Mohawks and glittering studs in their ears. A disgruntled taupe Persian done completely in corn rows lurked in silence on the back counter, and a friendly Maine Coon cat whose back half was bared in a classic French show poodle clip circulated at will, soliciting affection from any passing hands. The constant waving motion of the leonine flame of fur at the end of his bare tail was an unexpected plus. They called this a lion cut.

Tripod looked particularly exotic, his short smoky gray fur striated with a complex pattern that Corky had engraved on him with the narrowest trimmer; thin, parallel geometric lines of bare skin were painted bright blue. In this company, his missing leg seemed an accessory, like a hat worn at a rakish angle. ("No way are we gonna get into amputations," Corky had informed Hal when he stopped by to check on their progress and was particularly impressed with Tripod's new look. "Never say never," Hal had replied, busy directing the installation of their new sign.)

There was a black and white tom whose left side was shaved entirely bare, while the remaining fur on his right side sported a moussed henna rinse. (Lydia had to admit it looked better on him than it had that one time on her.) His naked side was mostly pink, with gray patches here and there, like continents on a map of some unknown world. Corky had left his whiskers and eyebrows when she shaved the left side of his face, giving him a fierce expression. Head on, he looked like a cross-section of a cat.

A plump female tabby with mackerel markings tried to remain dignified despite head-to-toe concentric rings of alternating shaved skin and bands of fur, which made her look like a child's idea of a raccoon. Lydia had painted her toenails blood red.

"I got a surprise for you," Corky said to Lydia when she was finished with the last cat, a half-grown orange kitten Corky had lured into her car behind the Stop & Shop when she'd gone out for supplies at mid-day. Taking a punchy suggestion of Lydia's literally, Corky had carefully shaved the letters D O G on one flank and otherwise ornamented him with a series of shaved and scissored hieroglyphic markings. The sculpted orange surface of his fur looked exactly like the expensive, wall-to-wall carpeting that Corky's great-aunt's neighbor had recently installed throughout his double-wide.

Corky and Lydia sat together in a relative silence for a moment, surveying their handiwork. Mozart concerti competed with the ceaseless Siamese dirge. It was like listening to two stations at the same time. Lydia held the concentric tabby in a hammerlock on her lap, waiting for the nail polish to dry.

"Surprise?" Lydia asked.

"Be right back." Corky got up and skipped into the tub room. Lydia tested the polish with a fingertip and relaxed her grip on the cat, which jumped down and began to wash vigorously. Lydia stretched her arms back over her head. This was a crazy thing to do, all of this; she had no idea what they would do if the party animals didn't sell, and all this effort and expense meant she would probably lose the shop a few months sooner than she would have otherwise. But this was fun. How about that? She was having a good time.

Corky returned, dangling a hamster cage in each hand.

"Look, Lydia hon. We got us some monogrammed mice—" She lifted up one cage and Lydia could see perhaps a dozen mice huddled together, each beautifully marked by an upper-case letter etched into its fur.

"And we got zodiac hamsters. Ta da!" Corky held out the other cage and Lydia peered inside at a wriggling heap of brown and white hamster flesh churning in a bed of cedar chips. "Hamsters were cheaper than gerbils, I hope that's okay. I know gerbils are more popular."

"You must have been up half the night," Lydia murmured, trying to take in Corky's handicraft. She had to admit that Corky seemed to have an incredible talent with the detailing clipper.

"Don't worry, they don't hold still so's you can see 'em but we got all twelve signs here. I copied 'em out of a book. *Linda Goodman's Sun Signs.* Wasn't she the one up and died? She musta known it was gonna happen, you think, Lydia?"

Lydia laughed. She was beginning to get Corky. "Corks, these are fabulous. I would never have thought of anything like this. You're really something. I mean it. You've got a terrific skill as well as imagination, did anyone ever tell you that?"

Corky poked her fingers through the cage wire to touch some of the hamsters. "That Pisces over in the corner was a bitch."

"The hamster, or the sign?"

"Oh, no, honey, I mean the actual whattayacallit, the insignia, whatever. It was hard to copy. These little cuties were just as agreeable as could be. Not like some others I could name, present company *included*," Corky emphasized, glaring at the Siamese trio.

A loud shave-and-a-haircut rapping at the front door signaled the arrival of Harold Blinder, Marketing Consultant. He bustled in, stopped dead in his tracks, swiveled around theatrically, and let out a long whistle of admiration.

"Ladies, I am overwhelmed," he said with drama, doffing an imaginary hat and sweeping it low. "This is incredible. You have nourished the seed I planted, and you have watered it, fertilized it, you have—"

"Corky gets most of the credit," Lydia interrupted, feeling the usual mix of fondness and irritation for this patter. In the past week the three of them had eaten supper together at Freddie's Flapjacks three times. There had been some serious conversation and some good laughs. Hal was basically okay. Even though he was at moments right at the edge of inappropriate with Corky, and he spoke perpetually like a freeze-dried instant marketing consultant to whom someone had just added water.

"She's the one with the gift, not me, Hal. I would still be clipping poodles by the book. This is really your baby, the two of you. But," Lydia added, "Please remember, Hal as in pal, we can't pay you a thing until we make some money, if we ever do."

"I have something else," Corky said, with hesitation. "I stopped at the mall for a little bit on my way over here. And I took these little guys in there with me."

"It's probably against the rules, though I suppose you could claim they're support hamsters. Did anyone see you? Did you get in trouble?" Lydia didn't want to be stuck with some stupid whopping fine for unauthorized hamsters.

"No, I mean yes, I guess a lot of people saw me. But I didn't get in trouble. I handed out a whole bunch of our new "Party Animals" cards. I hope you don't mind. I had just picked 'em up at the copy shop, and I know I should have checked with you. But I was afraid you would say no."

"That was a great idea," Lydia said. "You thought I would disapprove?"

"I guess it's time we both stop underestimatin' each other." Corky gave Lydia a shrewd look and continued. "So I gave a lot of the cards out, to some of those kids, the ones with the piercings and spikes and whatnot. Mall rats?"

"Go on." Harold Blinder was mesmerized.

"I had to ignore my heebie-jeebies, I admit. The black lipstick? And tattoos every whichaway? Those lip rings and the teeny chains from their ears to their noses? Ow! Then this one kid started in about tattoos on the animals. He gave me a card for a tattoo guy he says would maybe moonlight and do some work for us. But that's what I'm telling you—they all went wild over these little guys. That's what I want to tell you both. So I hope it's okay," Corky said with a worried look, shifting her gaze between Lydia and Hal. "I think I could have sold every one of these critters twice. But I knew we needed them for our grand opening. But what if they all show up here? All those kids?"

"Brilliant," pronounced Hal, awestruck. "Absotively, posolutely, a brilliant marketing strategy, right on target. You're a natural marketer! Corky, if you have any other ideas, I want you to speak right up."

"Well, I do have one more," Corky said unexpectedly. "Wait. Where did I put that bag?" She rummaged under the counter for a moment and brought out a plain brown paper sack that resembled a two-pound bag of sugar. She opened the top carefully, folded it back, and extended the bag. Lydia and Hal both looked inside.

"Glitter?" Lydia asked politely. She was a teenager, after all. "You want to decorate the place with that for the opening?"

"Glitter Litter," Corky replied.

"Unbelievable," whispered Hal. "Everything this woman says is gold. Pure gold."

"Wouldn't they track it around?" Lydia asked. "Wouldn't it get on their fur and then into their digestive systems?"

"Who cares if it gets tracked around? That's part of the deal, the effect, you know?" Corky replied. "But I went to see that vet—the one who did Tripod by mistake?—and he took a look at the stuff and he said it was anert? Inert? Is that the word? He said it wouldn't hurt 'em, it would just pass right on through and go back in the litterbox. So I was thinking we make our own bulk mix, you know, get a deal from the Agway on a ton of the cheapest litter? And put it in bags and make it our brand, and sell Glitter Litter by the pound."

"I am in the presence of greatness," Hal breathed fervently. "If I may make one very small suggestion."

"Jump right in," Corky invited.

"Small g, capital L See? Like this," Hal explained as he picked up a pen and drew **g-L-i-t-t-e-r** on a Party Animals invoice pad. "I think we can patent this and go national. I think I can find the investors, too." Hal's doughy face beamed with excitement. "We're talking big. I mean, *really* big. This is the big one! We can franchise Party Animals grooming parlors on the back of it. Big picture—it's going to make us rich, you know that, Lydia? Corky?"

Corky reached into the bag, grabbed a handful of the pink glitter, and lofted it into the air, shouting, "We're going to be rich!"

Lydia tried not to think about the everlastingness of glitter as it rained down all over everything. Or the dubious wisdom of Doctor Veterinary Amputations R Us. What the hell.

Enough underestimating! Away with melancholy! She dipped into the bag and tossed a handful up into the air, shouting, "You're a genius, Corky McDougal! You're a genius too, Harold Blinder!" She lofted another handful across the room. Several cats jumped down and began swatting at the beautiful fallout.

Hal scooped a double handful of the glitter and pitched it high. "We're all geniuses!" he crowed, as it rained down on them. "We're in the big leagues now!" he shouted, and for that moment, Lydia almost believed him.

Sunday, Upstate

IT WAS AFTER THEY PASSED the fourth gas station that Alice began to hum.

"Stop humming, will you?" Lloyd hated Alice's humming. He knew she hummed when she had something to say but had decided not to say it. Lloyd drove along the curving country road with precision and expertise, his left arm propped on the open window, his sleeves rolled up in two precise folds.

He kept downshifting to third gear on the curves, and then back up to fourth, and sometimes when he shifted he kept his left arm where it was on the edge of the window, abandoning the steering wheel for brief moments.

Alice stared straight ahead, searching the road for signs of impending civilization and more gas stations. The little stylized gas pump on the dashboard had been glowing urgently for almost twenty miles. More than half a gallon, she calculated. She could picture that last inch of gasoline splashing around in the tank. They had been on the outskirts of a small town when the amber light flickered on, and they had passed through the town, and now they were on a road all leafy and green and summery and probably not even zoned for gas stations.

In the back seat, Joanna and Ian wrangled over a kaleidoscope.

"You said it would be my turn after ten minutes. Give it! You *said*. You said. Didn't she, Mom? Didn't she? Please make her give it." Ian was two years younger and, at ten, almost comically serious. Alice thought he was the nicest boy she had ever encountered and could hardly believe he was hers, a member of this family. She wished she knew a way to tell him he was doomed to continuous frustration in all future dealings with girls like his complicated, condescending, and devious sister.

Alice turned around to adjudicate, but before she could say anything, Joanna tossed the kaleidoscope carelessly across the back seat, saying, "Here, have the baby toy, baby."

Ian picked it up and squinted into the eyepiece, rotating in a slow circle out his window. Joanna flounced and slumped in one motion, ignoring Alice's look of disapproval.

Alice turned around and took another peek at the odometer. Twenty-three miles on the perilously low tank. Lloyd drove with an air of satisfaction that seemed to come to him whenever he was behind the wheel of a car on a country road. Alice thought of the look on his face as his Honor Roll Student in the Country expression. I see things others overlook, it said. I am so sensitive and pleased to be alive, so appreciative of nature, so noticing, so intense, so thoughtful, and such a good driver, too.

"What?" He glanced at her in irritation.

"What, what?" she said, craning her neck slightly to see ahead as they rounded a curve, in hope of catching the first glimpse of a miraculous gas station.

They approached a large white house perched on a patch of lawn at a four-way stop. Alice wondered if the people in the house could tell them the distance to the next gas station. She supposed they must know. There was a card table heaped with burlap bags out front, with a painted sign propped against the front legs that said CORN. As Lloyd downshifted precisely toward the intersection, Alice wondered briefly if he was stopping to buy corn.

A swaybacked garage with the doors open stood next to

the house. In the moment they passed it, she could see a lawn mower, a red gasoline can, rakes and shovels in a row, and several tires, all ranked neatly along one wall to allow room in the garage for the pale blue Mercedes, a very old one, that was parked at an angle on the lawn, its trunk open.

They accelerated smoothly through the intersection and then down a hill. There were occasional farms, and after another mile they passed a weather-beaten sign for pies and eggs, but Alice didn't see a driveway or stand that went with the sign.

"Aren't you going to stop for gas?" she finally said, eyes straight ahead.

Lloyd shrugged and looked down at the dashboard.

"We can easily get 300 miles on a tank, and we've only gone a few miles with the light on. The way they make these gauges is ridiculous. It's just a gimmick. The light goes on when you have a quarter tank. Why do you always worry about things like that?"

"Why don't you ever worry about things like that?"

"You're the only person I know who would turn around and go home if you were to see one of those 'Road Legally Closed: Fines Doubled' signs on the highway," Lloyd retorted.

"Mom, can I go to the bathroom soon?" Ian interrupted. "It's not an emergency *yet*," he added, "but I also have a headache."

"Stop looking through the kaleidoscope and keep your window open, sweetie," Alice said. "You can go to the bathroom at the next *gas station*." Alice shot a look at Lloyd, who did not acknowledge the discussion.

"Why did you say it that way?" Joanna sat up. "Why did you say it that way?" she persisted. "At the next *gas station*," she parroted, in an unfortunately accurate mimicry of her mother's tone.

"Christ Almighty, we'll stop at the next gas station!" Lloyd shouted, annoyed by these disagreeable people in his car who were apparently incapable of enjoying the scenery and fresh air of open country the way he did.

They drove on in a thick, aggrieved silence.

It was at the crest of a hill, with a sweeping vista of farm-land falling away below, that the car began to cough and hes-itate. Lloyd floored the gas pedal, and the car lurched along for a few hundred yards more before the engine died, and for a moment they were rolling down a gentle slope in a perfect, peaceful parody of a Sunday drive.

Lloyd wrenched at the powerless steering wheel and the car glided onto the grassy shoulder of the road. He was able to brake gradually, and they eased to a graceful stop at a grassy clearing beside an old farm gate.

No one said a word.

Lloyd got out and shut his door with a careful *thunk*. He stretched elaborately, rolled down his shirt sleeves and but-toned his cuffs. He got his sweater out of what he insisted on calling "the boot" because that's what it was called in the owner's manual, lowered the lid carefully until the lock clicked, and then, as if he had been alone all this time, he walked away.

Once beyond the car, Lloyd slung his sweater over one shoulder and began loping in the more purposeful stride he used when he went walking for exercise in their neighborhood on weekends. Alice watched him in the rearview mirror. He looked completely intentional.

"Daddy has gone to get gas," Alice offered to her children. There was no sound from the back seat. She turned around. Both children were staring at her.

"How do you know?" asked Joanna.

"Don't be ridiculous, sweetheart," Alice replied carefully, evenly. "Ian, if you have to pee, you can go over there in those trees. There's nobody for miles around. Joanna? Do you have to go? Now's a good time."

Both children opened their car doors and hopped out.

It was a beautiful, nearly perfect afternoon. They slammed the doors and Alice leaned back and closed her eyes. After a while, she could hear their voices. They were playing a game of some kind, sitting on a fence. Alice was always relieved when they got along; it made her feel like a good mother.

She cranked her window open all the way and slid down in her seat, putting her knees up against the dashboard. She closed her eyes again.

As a child, Alice spent countless hours waiting in cars. Once, when she was about Ian's age, her father took her on a long drive to look at a summer house they might rent. She waited patiently while he was inside talking to the owner. When he finally did come out for her, she had fallen asleep. When he touched her shoulder and leaned in through the car window to kiss her forehead, she could smell the sweetness of his whiskey breath.

"Do you want to see it?" he had asked. She wasn't sure if this meant Do you want to see the house we're going to live in this summer? or Do you want to see the house because you'll never have a chance to see it again?

It was a typical upstate Victorian farmhouse, with porches and big cupolas on two sides. Like the perfect house in some dream Alice couldn't quite remember, it stood on a high grassy hill. Hand-in-hand, they climbed up some enormous and steep fieldstone steps cut into the hilly lawn and followed a path her father seemed to know that led them to a side porch. When they didn't go in, when her father sat her down on the bottom step and drew her to his lap, she knew then that they weren't ever going to live in this house.

Just one tear welled up and ran down her cheek. Alice slid off her father's lap and lay on the cool grass. She turned over, away from him. And over again. She rolled away from his brown shoes, away from the marvelous dream house. She rolled all the way down the hill, until the house and her father and the sky were just a spinning blur.

She lay at the bottom of the hill for a long time. When she sat up, she looked back at the porch steps, expecting to see her father sitting where she had left him. But he wasn't there. He was lying on the ground. He was rolling over and over. He was rolling down the hill. Alice wrapped her arms around her knees and squeezed them very tight and waited for her father.

Green Thumb

No one at the hospice knows my real name, but a lot of them call me the Plant Lady, and that's how I think of myself sometimes. I wear my Plant Lady apron with pockets for my pruners and scissors, and there's a cunning little loop on the right side for the plant misting bottle, which would be perfect if I were right-handed. The apron isn't really mine—it belongs to the Northbury Women's Garden Club. It's dark brown and much more masculine than anything I might have picked for myself, but Elsie Edwards ordered it from some catalogue and donated it when the Club voted to provide a volunteer for the hospice, and she's never been one for frilly florals. Her living room, which I see periodically because our meetings take place once a month in the homes of our members on a rotating basis (and as the Recording Secretary I attend every meeting), is very matchy-datchy, all solid yellows and blues.

I've never worn any kind of a uniform in my life, but there's something nice about getting out of my car every Wednesday and tying on the apron and walking in there with a purpose that anyone can see just from looking at me. I try to get there around eleven, so I'm not in the way of any doctors or blood-testing people, and I'm through before the lunch carts begin. I'm there for less than an hour, really, but it has given me something in the middle of my week to plan around.

I had a different routine when Duff was alive. I used to go

nearly every morning to the bookstore just a few blocks from my house, a pleasant walk, really, past a small park. At the store no one ever said Duff wasn't welcome, and he would sit beside me while I browsed and chose a category for the morning. I liked to straighten up the shelves and help keep the books organized, you see. I have no idea if the staff ever noticed the little jobs of straightening and rearranging that I did for them. It's a lovely store, with old wooden floors and lots of books, and nobody minds if you browse for hours, but I have to say it isn't the tidiest bookstore I have ever seen. One of the girls behind the counter would give Duff bites of her morning muffin. I haven't been back since, without him. I suppose there are books every which way, especially in the gardening section where so many people seem to browse without buying anything.

I agreed to keep up the club's obligation at the hospice until spring, since most of the older members don't like to go out on snowy days and I don't mind weather; living on my own, I've developed a lot of faith in front-wheel drive.

I would gladly go there more often, but the hospice people requested only one weekly visit, and the weekend nurses are supposed to water, though they forget sometimes. Even though twice a week would probably be better for the plants, once does seem to be sufficient. If a plant becomes sick or dried-out between visits, it's not very difficult to treat it. You can take your time with sick plants. You can replace the dead ones.

No ficus that ever dropped dead has broken your heart, which is more than I can say for every single cat or dog I have ever known. They all die on you, one way or another. Or they disappear and you never know what happened. And which is worse, anyway, dragging a dying Portuguese Water Spaniel that never harmed anybody off to chemotherapy week after week until the poor thing is practically begging for a visit from Dr. Kevorkian or wondering forever about an extremely

affectionate Maine Coon cat who one day simply stops showing up at the back porch for his supper?

I volunteered for the Garden Club job at the hospice after
Duff died just two months ago. He was a wise little Scottie,
and he had been my companion for ten years when he sick-
ened and then died very suddenly of a tumor on his liver. Its
size had doubled and doubled again in a matter of days and
had grown to the dimensions of a grapefruit, according to the
veterinarian. I haven't been able to bring myself to eat a grapefruit since then.

Medical people always compare growths to foods, for some
reason. Five years ago, when my gynecologist told me I needed
a hysterectomy, he said I had a scattering of fibroid tumors all
through my uterus "like someone had flung a handful of lentils in there." It was a disturbing picture, and I didn't like to
think of it. The pathology report, which Dr. Gilson offered
me at my follow-up visit and which I, for some unwise reason, read thoroughly, described some of the larger fibroids as
"bulging, whorled, and white," as if instead of the baby which
at one time in my life I thought I would surely have, I had
produced some sort of tumorous law firm. Of course, I haven't
eaten lentils since the operation.

I have developed a personal policy of avoidance of any de-
tailed conversations about other people's insides, because inevitably someone will have experienced a ghastly something the
size of a walnut or a grape or a plum, and it could be possible that someday I will end up on a diet restricted entirely to
things too large to be used for comparative descriptions of dis-
eased body parts.

The hospice is located at the edge of the highway in a converted warehouse in a strange, uninhabited part of town
known for concerns such as ladder factories and printing companies. It's very bright and airy inside, with a lot of glass and
very good light, which the plants appreciate. One reason I vol-

unteered for the job, frankly, was to get out of the house more, because I was afraid that I was beginning to hallucinate. On too-quiet afternoons I could hear the distinctive sleep-breathing sound of a Scottie in the corners of my bedroom. I know I heard his tags jingling to the door to greet me when I came in from shopping one morning. There were too many days when I glimpsed Duff for an instant—a sweater or my handbag, inevitably—on the sofa, by the arm that is stained just where he used to rest his dear little bearded snout. I couldn't return to the bookstore because the people there would expect to see Duff beside me, and I knew I couldn't bear those expectant glances, which would make me see, and then not see, my sweet Duff all over again.

The first time I walked into the hospice and saw the center atrium jungle of potted palms and ferns and ficus arranged attractively with a few benches, I thought it was like a very nice mall, only without fountains. Or shops, of course. But then I saw some of the patients, the ones who could walk around, and for a brief moment, it seemed like some sanitized, futuristic version of Auschwitz, the people in pajamas were so silent and cadaverous.

Every one of them has AIDS. That's entirely what this place is for. It's all government funding, and the patients are too poor to be anywhere else or they wouldn't be here, but it's quite a nice facility, really. I'm happy to think my tax dollars can do something good, and a place such as this really does give me hope that the New Deal hasn't been completely dismantled.

Most of the patients are a good deal younger than I am, and it just about breaks my heart to think about how it must be to face death in your twenties. I simply can't imagine it. But then, I can't really imagine being poor or a drug addict or a homosexual or a prostitute. Or Black, for that matter. (Not all Black people call themselves African-Americans these days.

My friend Mae, the woman who comes in and does things for me around my house twice a week, always says: What's Africa got to do with me who was born down in Vienna, Georgia, that's what I'd like to know?)

But I'm just there to tend to the plants, which I do briskly and efficiently, snapping off dead fronds and leaves, digging around in the soil to test the pH with a little kit, watering, and misting. I say hello to the patients—I know some of their names. Hello, Plant Lady, they say back. I am supposed to wear surgical gloves, which are available for the staff in boxes here and there and everywhere, but sometimes I forget. I always feel that when I put those gloves on I am insulting the patients, as if my wearing gloves signifies that I believe they are unclean. It's silly, anyway, because according to the newspaper articles I have read, both the patients and I would have to be engaging in extremely unsuitable behavior involving these plants in order for there to be any risk of disease transmission.

It's hard not to be self-conscious going through my routine because it's like a performance, as there are always patients watching me prune or pick off dead leaves or remove gum wrappers from the pots. I'm perfectly good at this. I have a green thumb, as they say, and plants grow for me. Sometimes some of the patients talk to me about the plants or about something on television. I get the feeling that a lot of them don't have any visitors except for people who come to provide services one way or another. I hadn't really wanted to get to know any of the patients because I don't want to become attached to any of them.

Then last month, when I was just about finished with the usual business, one of the patients asked me to do something for him. His name is Mike, and he's confused a lot of the time. His navigational skills are poor—I've seen him wandering into different patient rooms while tugging at his drawstrings, and it has made me nervous, as it seems evident at those moments that he's searching for the bathroom. He is always intercepted by one of the nurses before something unfortunate occurs, at least that is the case when I've been on the premises.

Could you water my plants for me?

That's what he said. He asked this in such a pleading tone that I couldn't just flat out refuse, though I confess that my first thought was that he was requesting in some euphemistic way that I assist him on a bathroom mission. Also, I wasn't sure about the protocol of entering a patient's room. I followed him through a doorway, though, half expecting that we were wandering randomly, but next to the bed there was a framed snapshot Mike had shown me over and over my first day at the hospice, of a healthy-looking Mike, with a mustache and a thick head of shoulder-length hair, grinning with a group of men on a fishing boat, each of them wearing identical caps from a local tire company.

Here are all of my plants, he said, enunciating slowly and awkwardly, as if he had rehearsed the line. He waved an arm in the direction of his windowsill. On the sill were a row of vases and baskets of dead flowers.

These are flowers, I said.

Will you water them, please?

I didn't know what to say. At their best, these cut flowers had been the terrible kind of ordered-over-the-telephone arrangements involving carnations and chrysanthemums, all of which were now shriveled and black against plastic-looking greens that had stayed bright.

There's no point, I said. These aren't plants. They're flowers. I mean, they used to be flowers, do you see? I pulled a handful of dead carnations on very short stems out of an ineptly anchored block of green foam and held it out towards Mike, who stepped back, shaking his head in refusal.

Man, those plants need watering real bad. That's why I'm asking you. Will you water my plants?

I can't water these, Mike, they're dead, I kept saying, as if we spoke the same language. They're dead flowers. Cut flowers. Don't you understand?

Then I cleaned up. I dumped each of those fetid arrangements into the trash, and I washed out the vases, which stank of halitosic flower-water. I left the empty vases and innocuous woven baskets, the sort that are made in China by unfortunate children earning pennies a day, on his windowsill.

Mike just sat on his bed staring at me. When I said goodbye, he didn't answer.

That night I dreamed about giant vines growing in my bedroom. (I am sophisticated enough about such things to recognize the sexual elements of this dream.) I tried to cut them with my pruning shears (I think I was wearing the Plant Lady apron but, embarrassingly, nothing else), but the vines were too thick and tough, and they grew longer and thicker before my eyes, snaking out the bedroom door and twining down and around the stair banisters. I woke then, almost tasting the words of the veterinarian on my tongue: this growth has doubled in size in a matter of days. I slept badly the rest of the night.

The next morning I went back to the hospice. I had never been there on a Thursday before, and it felt strange. I wasn't wearing my apron, of course, and as I approached the nurses' desk, I could tell that the two women who always greeted me warmly on Wednesdays didn't recognize me without it. One got up and walked away, adjusting her cardigan sweater over her shoulders with that universal gesture of nurses, and the other one snapped her gum and scowled down at paperwork.

I was carrying a Christmas cactus from my house, one that looked as if it would be blooming very soon.

This is for Mike, I said, putting it on the counter.

Mike's gone, the woman said without looking up.

I couldn't believe it. My hands began to tremble.

What do you mean? I said finally, after a long silence that she didn't seem to notice or participate in.

He ain't here. He's gone, she said again.

What do you mean by gone? Did he—Did he—I couldn't say it.

She looked up at me then and recognized me. Oh, it's you. Hi. She looked puzzled. Mike ain't here on Thursdays. He's never here. Thursdays are his rehab day. He goes with the van downtown to the bottle place. He sorts. Seeing the series of looks that must have crossed my face while she spoke, the nurse opened her eyes wide and nodded with sudden comprehension.

Oh no, honey, you thought I meant he was *gone*, like really *gone*. She snorted a brief, mirthless laugh. No, most everyone do go from this place, but when they go, they don't go in the rehab van, I can tell you that. Mike and them will be back by four.

I'm still the Plant Lady, but my heart has gone out of it. Mike loved the cactus, he told me the following Wednesday, but he missed his flowers. He looked wistfully towards the row of empty vases and baskets when he said this, and I was stung by his sweet forgiveness of my terrible mistake. The Wednesday after that, he had developed pneumonia and was on oxygen and couldn't leave his bed, so we just waved and he pointed towards the sill at the cactus, which had bloomed with one small red flower, and he gave me a thumbs up.

The following Wednesday, after I had finished my routine, when I put my head around Mike's door the first thing I saw was a vase of withered sweetheart roses and a small Chinese azalea plant in a plastic pot on the sill instead of the cactus and the empty vases and baskets. Mike was sitting on his bed with his back to me, but when he turned his head, he was a gaunt young woman in a seersucker robe, tethered to an intravenous drip, her head wrapped tightly in a scarf or a bandage,

I'm not sure which. She turned her head and looked at me over her shoulder, like the girl in the Vermeer painting, and I knew Mike was really gone.

I've told the Garden Club that someone else will have to take over for me sooner than I thought, even before the weather gets milder. Elsie Edwards has a Range Rover, after all. It's not that I don't like doing the work. I just can't bear to form any more attachments right now. Maybe, in a while, when it warms up, I'll think about a puppy.

Channel-Surfing
with the Treatment Team

Holographic manuscript (pencil, unsigned, no date) on multiple lined sheets from a legal-sized pad, found folded inside a copy of TV Guide *dated September 14–20, 1985, removed from a heating duct during demolition of the River Edge Treatment Facility in Northbury, Connecticut in summer 2018*

I GET THE CLICKER because it's Tuesday. On Tuesdays, Mikey Osborne isn't here because he has an appointment at seven o'clock with the director. Usually, by the time Mikey comes back, our shows are over. On other nights, and on Tuesdays when his appointment doesn't last as long as usual, Mikey gets the clicker.

My regular appointment with the Director is on Monday at four o'clock. I am brought back to the house in time for dinner—psychotics and schizophrenics eat a great deal more than other people—and after that we line up for meds from someone on the treatment team. Monday is usually Don Hope. When he's not here, someone invariably points out that we are "Hope-less." Psychotics and schizophrenics pun a lot more than other people.

The rest of the treatment team: Alex Gold, Tracy Sternbergen, Isaac Johnson—he's black and used to be a catatonic; now he's a social worker and just very quiet—and Dodd Fletcher.

The member of the treatment team I like best is Dodd. He's from one of those aristocratic families that has so many last names they use them for first names too; his full name is Doddsworth Livingston Fletcher III. When I hear the others call him Dodd, and when I hear myself, it sounds to me like a bunch of bluebloods with boarding school lockjaw saying "Dad."

Monday night is *Golden Palace* at eight. "The women are thrilled to see Dorothy until they learn she expects Sophia to go home with her. (Part 1 of 2)." I vote for a movie, *Better Off Dead*, but am overruled by the overmedicated majority who are always anxious to please the sadistic, manipulative, tasteless minority of one, Mikey Osborne. He holds the clicker like a gun and shoots from the hip. Sometimes he puts the clicker right up against the dandruffy temple of Owen McNabb, who smiles a little smile and keeps up his humming mumble even when Mikey pulls the trigger and says, "You're dead meat, man," to Owen. Through Owen's skull, a channel dies.

Mikey channel-surfs during commercials, and sometimes the group gets so engrossed with something on another station that there's a fight about what we're actually watching. In the interest of harmony, Alex, or Tracy, or Dodd usually watches with us, or at least lurks nearby, watching us watch whatever it is that we're watching. Isaac and Don hate channel-surfing and won't allow it on their nights. Period. End of story. The others tolerate it, but barely. So the new house rule is: Channel-surfing, if at all, only with a member of the treatment team.

Strangely, an hour later, on another channel, a completely different *Better Off Dead* is playing, but I am hardly going to be satisfied with "Two women reach beyond their differences to form a life-altering friendship," when the *Better Off Dead* that started opposite *Golden Palace* was "A love-sick teenager has a difficult time dealing with his decidedly eccentric family

and the fact that his girlfriend has left him for another guy."
No offense, but that's entertainment.

Tuesday is another story. *Carry on Screaming*, for one thing.
"Ghouls, monsters, mad scientists and vampires inhabit a lone
house in the forest and busy themselves by turning people
to stone." Crank that sound up! Mid-flick, the screams from
the television set—an old Sony donated by somebody's family
(the somebody isn't here anymore; the somebody killed himself in a room at the Y last Christmas)—almost drown out
the screams from the Day Room, where Jane Kavetsky goes
to smoke and sometimes, perchance, to scream.

"Reduction, please?" Dodd puts his head around the door
to the Chambre de Television, aka Tuber City, aka The Wreck
Room. He smokes a meerschaum, and keeps the stem clamped
between his teeth (just like dear old granddad Fletcher, no
doubt, and probably dear old grandmother Fletcher, too, on
the Livingston-Biddle side). He points through the glass doors
of the Day Room at Jane, who is screaming in short, almost
conversational bursts, while pacing and waving her hands in
front of her as if to brush away huge cobwebs, and then he
twirls his fingers near his temple.

"You mean, crazier than the rest of us?" asks Jennifer Wald-
man, an anorexic poet with several sets of amateurish slash
marks on her wrists. Her insurance has almost run out, and
she'll have to leave in three days. She has been holding a single piece of popcorn between her thumb and forefinger all
evening, while everyone else has scrabbled the communal
bowl down to Orville's little failures and a slick of resolidi-
fied margarine.

By way of changing the subject, Dodd begins singing
"Whoop Daddy Ooden Dooden Day," around the meerschaum, and we all shush him. "Go busy yourself turning
people to stone," I call out obscurely, feeling very good indeed
about that bit of cleverness which no one but Owen catches.

Someone throws a throw pillow—psychotics and schizophrenics are very literal-minded—and Dodd ducks around the door-
frame as the pillow whizzes past. I turn the sound down two
clicks. Jane turns it down two clicks, too.

After *Carry on Screaming*, we're entitled to another half hour
of viewing pleasure before lights out. I ought to run a wash
tonight, so my treatment team review meeting on Thursday at
three o'clock won't consist entirely of an analysis of my inabil-
ity to wear clean, or even clean-ish clothes more often, but I
can't face the basement of earthly delights, and decide that
tomorrow is another day here at the Edge. I check the listings
in *TV Guide*. So little to choose, so much time. I balance the
clicker in my hand with my personal and unique mixture of
insouciant pleasure in and contempt for that which we receive
as popular culture over today's airwaves.

Hockey Week? 700 Club? Amazing Live Sea Monkeys? No and
no and no. But here we go. Do I demonstrate leadership potential with my peers or what?

I hold the clicker at the ready, waiting for the last of *Carry
on Screaming* to unfurl. Our favorite, "To Be Announced,"
is next.

The View from the 99th Floor

PHILIP ASKED IF I wanted to see a great view of the city, a secret view he had discovered, a view nobody else knew about or had ever seen. It was a typical offer, one of our treasure hunt challenges. We often set riddles and dares for each other, with mystery destinations. This was an adventure for a cold winter night, nearly fifty years ago, something a little risky, actually dangerous, something very us. Even though there was no us. I was eighteen, he was nineteen. We weren't boyfriend and girlfriend. We had something even better, even closer, a friendship that had skipped over courtship and romance, and sex, and gone straight to comfortable, old-married-couple finishing each other's sentences and interrupting and mind-reading and bickering. We had a pact that if all else failed by age forty, we would marry each other.

Philip was from Oregon, from a town where doctors and lawyers rode mountain bikes to work. He regarded all of New York City as if it were a national park. He was a precociously talented graphic design student at Cooper Union, living in a tiny, obsessively neat fourth-floor walk-up studio on Seventh Street in the East Village, two doors down from McSorley's Ale House, where women had finally been "allowed" in the door only a couple of years before. Every day he carried his bicycle up and down those stairs. He had painted the apartment with expensive paint that was the whitest possible

white, and the only thing hanging on any of those walls was
that bicycle.

Philip had a girlfriend, a Parsons fashion design student
whose internship as an assistant to a famous couture designer
known for outrageous red carpet glitz somehow required that
she herself only ever wore black turtlenecks and jeans. Philip's
relationship with her was inexplicable and beside the point.
Beside my point, and also, it seemed, beside Philip's. Neither of us took her very seriously. Our secret nickname for her
was Goo-Goo Eyes, the name by which she was known to us
before either of us knew her real name, which was Lisa. Our
horrifying snideness was very us. The name Goo-Goo Eyes
had come from Philip's sister, a lawyer who took us both out
for dinner when she was in New York for a meeting. Later
that night, when we had dropped in at a large Cooper Union
party in the East Village, she had observed Lisa's clear infatu-
ation with Philip from across the room. Philip, his sister, and
I spent the party lurking in a corner and drinking bad sangria
(I am not sure I know of any other kind) while making ironic
comments and inventing nicknames.

Lisa was pretty in a wholesome, Midwestern, big-faced
way. She shopped for "grosheries" and periodically served a
Midwestern delicacy she called Tater Tot hot dish, a family
recipe she assembled with ground meat and canned peas and
cream of mushroom soup, which emerged from the invariably
teeny, filthy ovens in her various apartments, the top crunchy
layer of Tots fused together in neat rows. Lisa kept moving.
She moved from one unsatisfactory apartment to another, and
I was often enlisted to help, because I had an old Volkswagen
Squareback with sufficient cargo space to transport her rolled
mattress, her milk crates, and her old lady plaid suitcases from
each grim little studio to the next. Did she know I only provided those moving services as a favor to Philip? Probably it
helped her not mind my chronic presence in Philip's life.

Lisa stayed in the tiny, quaint, street-level Gay Street studio only a month, disliking the way tourists habitually peered in and studied her as if they were window shopping, unless she kept the curtain closed, depriving herself of daylight. The third-floor walk-up over a restaurant on Hudson Street had rats and she lasted there only two nights. Worldly and patient, I helped pack her up to move once more. Finally, Lisa was satisfied with an alcove studio on the tenth floor in a white brick building on 15th Street inhabited by secretaries and flight attendants and bank tellers. There was a doorman. The clanking of the elevator door opening and closing directly across the hall didn't seem to bother her, though it set my teeth on edge whenever I was in her office-like apartment for one of those Tater Tot hot dish nights. This anodyne apartment with its steel doorframes and low ceilings and beige carpeted floors was home at last. Philip and I didn't conceal our contempt for Lisa's preference for ordinariness.

Our mutual condescension for Lisa was one of the many strange threads that bound us together. Sometimes it just felt fun, the two of us being smug and superior, speaking our private language—evidence to me that Philip and I had something far more intense, more intimate, than whatever it was they had. Sometimes I felt guilty, though, uneasy, as if we had been getting away with something that could abruptly crash if emotional reality ever dawned on Lisa.

I was working in an architecture office on 57th Street by day, ghostwriting text for a book for a famous big-ego architect known equally for his white buildings and for his unwillingness to share design credit with his staff, and I was taking night classes at The New School, working slowly towards a college degree I never did obtain. I was an independent eighteen-year-old, proud to the point of obnoxiousness about my independence and precociousness. Having left Northbury,

Connecticut, at sixteen (a freshman year of college after eleventh grade my ticket away from an unpleasant family life that has no bearing on this story), I was living in a somewhat nicer if less gleaming apartment than Philip's, since my bathtub was in the bathroom and not the kitchen, on Waverly Place, just west of Washington Square.

I was living on my own at this point, since the departure of Janis, a difficult roommate who wrote her initials obsessively on everything in the apartment that was hers, including certain eggs, though she always denied eating my un-personalized sardines and Triscuits, which she devoured as fast as I could replenish my designated side of the kitchen pantry shelf. She had finally moved out, choosing a leap into a non-standard living arrangement with a married couple, having fallen in love with them both. Did they all share their eggs? She took my bathmat.

My own situation had its non-standard aspects; at this time I was in an obsessive romance with Jack, a charming and unreliable poet of thirty-five who arrived and disappeared from my life at unexpected intervals. Although the bathmat had matched my towels, I missed nothing else about Janis, especially not the heartfelt monologues she called discussions that circled endlessly around boundary issues and eating disorders without ever landing.

Philip and I began our mystery expedition when it was already very late and very dark and very cold, close to midnight on that frigid January night. Of course, he had not told Lisa a thing about this outing, though they had gone to dinner together, which made it a little bit of a conspiracy, and all the more appealing. It was the kind of cold New York City winter night with a rime of frost everywhere, encasing everything in its glittering diamond skin, the kind of cold that forms sharp, icy specks in the air that hurt your lungs in a satisfying way when you draw a deep breath.

We walked south, through Little Italy and then through Chinatown, and as we trudged farther downtown and the streets grew less well-lit and less populated, I asked Philip to give me a hint about where we were heading, but he wouldn't tell me anything. I granted him this power. Sometimes I was the one with the power, as when I revised all of his writing, and knew more about history and politics, or took him to see a tapestry at The Cloisters (he had never heard of the Cloisters), or, one time, late one night when he had come to my door, sidling painfully, and I was able to provide him, gaze averted, the soothing unguents he desperately needed to extinguish the blistering itch of the poison ivy rash that was inexplicably all over his ass. He could never have gone to Lisa with this. We knew each other with an ease and familiarity neither of us had with anyone else, and we trusted each other.

We traipsed along, further and further south through the then-desolate streets of industrial Soho. I trusted Philip that this secret expedition would be worth my while. I was wearing a parka and gloves, but my face was practically immobilized by the cold, my thighs were frozen in my jeans, and my toes were growing numb in my ridiculous Frye boots, which I wore incessantly in those years. Who didn't? Only the Swedish clog people.

We stopped at a first destination on the way to wherever Philip was leading me, a massive construction site that occupied an entire city block. Philip knew exactly where we could slip through a gap in the loosely-chained plywood doors cut into the enclosure. It was a giant pit, a vast excavation in preparation for some immense construction project. We climbed down to the bottom, which took a long time, picking our way in deep frozen muddy ruts, and finally we were in the center of this earthen bowl, gazing up at the mostly dark looming office towers that rimmed the site.

"This is the view a cockroach has in your kitchen sink!" Philip shouted into the darkness, wheeling around, his arms extended, a cheerful twirling cockroach. Was this it, then? I tried to appreciate the drama of the setting, tried to see it through his eyes. Secret view? We had come a long way for this big pit of nothing. No, not at all, we still had a distance to walk. This was in fact the exact opposite of where we were headed. Had I no faith?

We climbed out, sliding on the frozen muddy bulldozer ramps. It was that much later, and colder, and darker. We trudged on. At this point I had absolutely no idea where we were or where we could be going. Perhaps we were headed for the very southern tip of Manhattan, the South Street Sea-port? One of the tall ships? Were we going to walk over a bridge to Brooklyn? I hoped not. My sense of time was frozen along with everything else. I didn't want to stop and fish out my watch from under my parka. I wore a small silver pocket watch on a chain in those days, a brief experiment of an affec-tation. That ended the day I saw a woman in the middle courtyard at the New School who not only also wore a pocket watch on a chain just like mine—she also wore a deerstalker cap and smoked a meerschaum pipe. Yikes.

I had no idea we had finally arrived at our destination, sev-eral blocks later, until Philip steered me to a halt at the edge of another vast, walled-off construction site. It was impossible to see where we were, and it was impossible to look up under the construction canopies that sheltered the adjacent sidewalks. Where were we? The only signs around us now were those identifying the various construction companies and engineers, and safety warnings, and numerous severe No Parking Active Entrance exhortations.

Philip said he had been here the night before and had dis-covered a way into the site. I followed him, wriggling through a gap in a chain link fence which he held for me as I wedged myself through, covering with his gloved hand the spiky wire that had snagged his parka, to protect mine. Knowingly, Philip then proceeded to flip aside the loose edge of a piece of plywood draped with a blue tarp, and together we squeezed through a second barrier of chain link fence and plywood. There were very few lights, just a scatter of lit caged safety bulbs hanging here and there, but my eyes adjusted to the darkness as I followed Philip's confident shape ahead of me. Now we were entering an open concrete building that seemed like a parking garage, making our way up an unfinished dark concrete stairway, a flight, another flight, another flight, the stairs lit only every few floors by a single bulb dangling here and there from snaked orange plastic electrician's work lamps. Sometimes we were climbing the stairs in nearly total darkness. Philip could have brought a flashlight.

Where the hell are we? I asked at about the twentieth floor. Philip grinned over his shoulder. We kept going up, and up. The stairwell was enclosed, though the raw concrete was unfinished, and I could only sense that we were in some office tower under construction. Each floor had a locked fire door. We climbed stairs and more stairs. A very tall office tower. Another flight and another. We settled into a wordless rhythm. It was hypnotic, exhausting, exciting, dangerous. Surely a crime. The air was raw with the fresh concrete of the stairwell, steel, freshly cut lumber. Floor numbers were spraypainted like graffiti on the concrete walls every few floors. Above the fiftieth floor, we were past the locked doors. The stairs were open on two sides, as the partition walls weren't finished, and there were stacks of drywall piled high.

We climbed on. By the seventieth floor the building's skin was incomplete, with two sides open to the frigid night air. Thick plastic sheets flapped in the wind where they weren't perfectly tacked to the beams they shrouded. My lungs were burning, and I was gasping for air. Stairs and stairs, an infinity of stairs. The cold of the concrete radiated through the soles of my absurd cowboy boots. My feet were blistering. I never wore those boots again.

There was a hint of dawn in the air when we got as far as

we could go, when we ran out of finished stairs at a spray-painted 99. Climbing higher would have meant balancing on open scaffolding. There were no partitions at all, not even stacks of drywall. The climb had taken the entire night, and we had never stopped except for a sudden freeze, no movement, don't make a sound, for several paralyzing minutes somewhere in the eighties, when we thought we heard footsteps coming up below us. But nobody came up the stairs or called out. There was a single guard, Philip had told me at the start of our climb, who was stationed in the construction trailer every night, and he made rounds every so often, but he stayed at ground level.

That was the only moment when I was not certain we were the only souls in the entire structure, which moaned eerily when the wind blew through the gaps in the unfinished structure. Standing there, trying not to gasp for air, listening for the footsteps of the guard who may or may not have been coming up the stairs behind us, I listened to the primeval sound of the night wind forcing itself through the interstices of the building, like a glorious version of the note you can play when you blow across the top of your soda bottle. I want to hear that note again. I have never heard that note again. I will never hear that note again.

At 99 we stopped climbing. The next flight was beyond a taut blue tarp. I was relieved when Philip didn't have a plan to crawl past it to keep climbing. He said we were as close to the top as we could safely go, though surely we had left "safely" behind long before this moment. We picked our way across the open concrete floor that ended at infinity, at nothing, it ended in the sky, it ended with Manhattan and sky and stars pressing against the cold air. I drew back, though we were a good twenty feet from the edge, discovering a fear of heights I hadn't known I possessed until that moment. (It has stayed with me, though.) There was only a bracing of vertical steel beams crossed by simple planks to mark the edges, to mark the difference between standing here on the 99th floor and falling through space, sailing away into the abyss that is New York City which was staring back at me.

What is this? Where are we, seriously?

Look over here, Philip said, steering me into a turn. I clutched his arm tightly while resisting movement. I didn't want to leave the safety of the vast middle of the open space, and he understood, swiveling me all the way around, slowly, counterclockwise, in place. It was almost like dancing. We were alone in our world. The glittering Hudson River. New Jersey. The Statue of Liberty. The bridges spanning the East River to Brooklyn. The Chrysler Building, the Empire State Building. The Hudson and New Jersey again. As we slowly turned, I saw the dark outline of an adjacent skyscraper, a solid mass, its glass wall reflecting the dark shadow of this building.

What is this? Really—tell me! Where are we?

It's the World Trade Center, Philip said. Look, there's the other tower. This is the South tower. The other one's already finished, so we can't get in. I mean, we probably could, but I think it would be a felony, breaking and entering. This is still a construction site, so if they catch us here we're just dumb kids wandering, not exactly breaking in.

We stared at the other tower. Dim interior lights punctuated its opaque darkness. I had never heard of the World Trade Center.

Reaching the 99th floor didn't feel like a particular triumph so much as the end of something endless. I was limp with fatigue. My hands were shaking. I was cold all the way through, and my clothes, soaked with chilling sweat, were as wet as if I had fallen through the ice on a pond. My teeth chattered uncontrollably as we gazed at the vast view of glittering, magnificent New York, framed by steel beams and flapping plastic. It was a higher up view than anyone else's.

Our secret view for now. It was something strange and thrilling, being up here where nobody was supposed to be. It was
very us. We knew things nobody else knew. We were a pair,
Philip and I, and at this moment we were truly looking down
on everyone else, from here to infinity. I knew I would never
do something like this again, glad as I was to have done it.

Philip hugged me, noticing how cold I was. I hugged him
back. We clung together. I knew you could do it, he said.

You knew you could talk me into it, I corrected him. You
may have to carry me down.

We should come back here, he said.

Yeah, sure, okay, for our wedding when we're forty, I agreed.

Deal, he said.

We held each other closer and more seriously than we ever
had before. It suddenly felt real, no longer a game, our shtick.
We were on a dangerous precipice, and we needed to take a
step back. Neither of us said anything more. The moment
passed, we moved apart.

From that moment on, we kept moving apart until we hardly
spoke from one month to the next. Philip took a job on a project in London and never got back in touch when he returned.
Jack the unreliable poet did me the favor of disappearing from
my life. Two years after this I would marry the man to whom
I am still married. We have children—two daughters who are
twice as old as I was on that cold winter night—and we have
grandchildren. Lisa was still living in that beige apartment,
according to the Manhattan phone book, so I sent a wedding
invitation, and Lisa and Philip showed up at our wedding.
They never gave us a wedding present. I never saw either of
them again, not for many years, until I ran into Lisa on First
Avenue, when I was on my way to meet a friend.

Lisa was pushing a classic rich person's baby carriage that
held a sleeping blonde child tucked under a pretty blanket.
We recognized each other simultaneously. She was wearing

pearls. Lisa told me that she and Philip had broken up right after the wedding, and that she was married to a banker and didn't need to work. She lived on Sutton Place. She was on the way to a park rendezvous with other mothers from her Lamaze group, so we only had that brief moment together on the corner, as we waited for the light to change.

Lisa told me she had thought of me not so long before our chance encounter, when she had glimpsed the unreliable poet. He was in a green uniform, riding the back of a garbage truck, swinging down to empty trash cans and then swinging back up. She laughed triumphantly when she told me about Jack's fate. Neither of us had been in touch with Philip. We both knew that he had made a name for himself in the past twenty years doing something with animation and computers on the west coast.

Does he remember that night? Did he think of it as I did, in the days after September 11th when the news was filled with so many images of firefighters going up those stairs, passing the throngs of office workers streaming down, in that stairwell? Does he recall it the same way, the night we stood so close together, gazing down at the city, the night our friendship or whatever it was culminated in that private, secret, triumphant ascent? The arduous cold and dark descent lay ahead of us, but for that moment, we had everything worked out, we knew so much, we had our lives ahead of us, and we were, it seemed, on top of the world.

Safe

THE RED BUTTON SO APPEALING, like a clown's nose waiting to be honked. The wooden steps so inviting, like a ladder waiting to be climbed. The exciting music, frantic and falsely cheerful, but with that hysterical pitch which on television always signifies something about to go wrong.

The red button so intriguing.

The little girl hated the man in the dirty green t-shirt who ran the Twister. He got to push the red button each time the ride stopped and started. That was his whole job, and it should be fun, he should love his job, but he was so bored and far-away, like the unsmiling school bus driver whose bus passed her house every morning, the one who never, ever waved back. The red button was so big and smooth-looking under the fingers of bad, green t-shirt man. His cigarette dangled between his lips and a curl of greasy smoke hung in the air in front of his scowly face. He smelled.

She knew he smelled because this was the second time she had ridden the Twister, all alone because she was a big girl of six and her mother didn't like rides much anyway. The first time, when he had bent over her to adjust the safety bar, she had accidentally breathed in a nasty whiff of armpit. Now, after some obligatory rides on the silly little junior roller coaster and the babyish merry-go-round, she was back on the Twister, an experienced adventurer adjusting the safety bar all by herself to pre-empt further assistance from bad smelly green t-shirt man.

As she had earlier, the girl's mother waited under a tree where it was shady and she could hold the girl's silvery balloon and watch her going around and around and around. It was beginning. Slowly at first, a teasing lazy few turns around. A mild little ride, nothing at all to be afraid of. But then more and more speed, more and more spinning, as the Twister uncoiled and recoiled its armloads of frenzied, screaming passengers. Around and around, each time they passed the big tree the girl turned her head against the force to look for her waving mother streaking by, until the Twister whirled too fast and her mother became an indistinguishable element of the motion-striped blur.

Each time she spun past the control platform, green t-shirt man was there leaning on the railing staring at nothing. As the coiled arm of the Twister flung each car out and then gathered it back in, the girl was suspended for a motionless moment directly over him. She could see the big flat red button next to his bored hand.

Green t-shirt man was dirty, but his red button was clean and smooth and the little girl really wanted to touch it.

The ride slowed disappointingly and then came to a stop, the way it always did, even though you hoped it would keep going, even though you were ready to get off and wobble away in the real, unspinning world. Some cars continued to swing around their off-center pivot, others were already fixed at an angle. She tried to predict where her car would stop and was almost right. The music insisted that everything was thrilling and wonderful but just wait. Green t-shirt man walked around popping open safety bars. In his wake, kids erupted out of the seats and scampered towards the exit steps, sneakered feet squeaking and thundering on the painted boards.

Grown-ups didn't usually need his help, but a fat lady wedged into a car over on the other side seemed unable to raise her safety bar and he ambled over to help her.

The red button was all alone and the girl was standing on

the top step for the exit, right next to it, only a thin drooping plastic link chain between them. Just a touch. Just to feel for a moment if it was as smooth as it looked.

Ducking under the chain, she stayed bent over and walked two steps still bent shorter than the chain droop, and then she straightened up to stand all the way tall in front of the red button. It glowed beautifully, like a sucked cough lozenge.

Green t-shirt man was now standing right there, right on the other side of the chain, and any second he would yell at her, but he never noticed her, and with his back still turned to the little girl he lifted open the big latch and swung the spring-loaded gate wide on the entrance ramp. Kids stampeded onto the platform, racing to claim seats.

"Sweetheart!" Her mother's voice was far away, all the way on the other side of the Twister. Green t-shirt man would turn around any moment.

She reached up and touched the red button. With just her fingertips. It was warm from the sun. It felt nice, the way her mother's pearls felt, neck-warmed, when she was allowed to play with them sometimes, for just a few minutes, at bedtime.

"Hey! Kid! Don't touch that!"

Green t-shirt man's unexpected crawly dirty touch on the back of her neck made her jump.

Her hand splayed on the red button, pressing down for just an instant.

The Twister came to life, turning, twisting, grinding.

Screams and screams and screams.

Green t-shirt man smashed his fist down on the red button just as her mother grabbed her under both arms and dragged her roughly down the wooden steps, away from the platform. She had not seen her mother fly up into the air right over the Twister to come and save her so fast.

Slung over one of her mother's shoulders, the little girl was bouncing too hard to see. Everyone was yelling to everyone else, and there were blurry people shouting and running in all directions. She shut her eyes, feeling all through her the harsh jolting of the pounding feet, the pounding heart—her own? Her mother's?

The little girl's lower lip was cut repeatedly by the corrugated sharpness of her new front teeth as her mother ran. She felt the blood pooling under her tongue and she opened her mouth to let it escape. Like Hansel and Gretel in the forest, they left a trail behind them. Would the green t-shirt man follow the blood drops and catch them? She was afraid of him. She began to cry.

At their car, the mother deposited the girl in the back seat. Was she crying, too? Her breath sobbed in and out of her as she bent over to lower the child onto the seat. The mother's blouse was patched with sweat. The girl didn't like it that her mother smelled different than she ever had before. It seemed bad, like something broken that could never be fixed.

The music, grinning and mean, seemed to follow them down the road. As they turned onto the main highway towards home, an ambulance going at top speed in the opposite direction passed them, siren blaring, lights flashing. The little girl sang a matching siren song under her breath until it faded.

"Hungry, sweetheart?" Her mother was looking at her in the rearview mirror, trying to catch her eye. There had been a plan to have hot dogs at the amusement park, and then cotton candy from the lady who wound it just so on the paper wand, conjuring the pink shreds like magic from the whirling invisible sugar cloud inside the metal bowl.

The girl shook her head no and looked away. Her tears had dried on her face with the blood from her bottom lip, and there was a coppery taste in her mouth. She was suddenly so tired. Where was her balloon? Gone.

"Me neither," the mother said softly. They drove in silence and the girl fell asleep.

When she woke, she was in her own bed, and her mother was sitting beside her in the semi-darkness.

"You won't remember this," her mother whispered. "It will be like a dream for you. We'll never go back to Northbury. They'll never find us. Never. You'll be safe."

That night the girl dreamed about the green t-shirt man. The red button was on his belt buckle, and he took hold of her wrist and forced her to touch it, over and over, and it glowed hotter and hotter until her fingers were burning and all he did was laugh, even though it hurt and nothing was funny. When she tried to push away from him, her trapped hand just kept pressing the red button harder and harder, while he laughed his mean laugh. When she woke up in the morning, it was raining and her mother was opening and closing drawers all through the house, packing everything.

Tiny Stapler

THIRTY-TWO YEARS AGO I was sent by the Smithers Employment Agency to interview with the worst client in the history of the agency. Four other girls had been rejected that same day, each one of them returning within an hour, in tears (poor Rose O'Brien couldn't stop sobbing for the longest time and Mary Casey went home with a migraine and never returned). Although I had very little experience as a personal secretary, in fact, none at all, having sold gloves at Saks for ten years until I was replaced by someone prettier though thoroughly unqualified, and even though Mr. Smithers had commented unfavorably on my unfortunate tendency to blush and stammer when flustered, which he said would make it hard to place me, I suppose he had run out of prospects to send.

So over to Dr. Marjorie Grimstone's I went, on the crosstown bus, wearing my three-button dove-gray cashmere gloves with my navy suit. Dr. Grimstone showed me her office as if I were a mental defective ("This is my office"). There was a small desk ("This is where you would sit and do your work on Tuesday and Thursday afternoons"), bare except for a telephone, a plastic-hooded adding machine, a large, gun-metal tape dispenser, and a tiny stapler ("I prefer the smaller staples for my patient notes and billing files; if operated precisely it won't jam"). Next to the desk loomed a massive IBM Selectric typewriter, shrouded in plastic, on its own typing table.

Dr. Grimstone sat me down on the hard stenographer's chair which rolled around on a plastic mat protecting her Turkish carpet, and then she sat across the room on a small, tufted arm-chair at the end of her analytic couch and tried to intimidate me by asking all sorts of rude personal questions, which she explained she was entitled to ask because she was a "shrink," as she put it. I came to see over time that Dr. Grimstone treated everyone this way, as if she had a special privilege to regard all of humanity as her research subjects. I don't really know why, but I stood up to her and I didn't cry like the others, or blush or stammer, even when she asked me if my orgasms were cli-toral or vaginal. Instead, I looked her in the eye and said Dr. Grimstone, I am your last chance at hiring a part-time sec-retary from the Smithers Agency, and even though I am not very experienced, I believe I can do the job, and you seem like someone capable of being kind, so why don't you just hire me and stop being so unkind, and she did.

By the time she died, Dr. Grimstone had a very organized estate. She was meticulous about the tiniest things: the Chinese porcelain, the Tupperware, the Turkish carpets, the extension cords, the family silver, the finger bowls, the Murano glass animals, the psychoanalytic journals. The shredding of patient records we had done together once she had become deaf as a post and couldn't keep asking patients to repeat their deepest secrets, to shout them out from that scratchy olive green couch under the Dürer woodcuts which had been her father's, which she left to the great-niece she liked best.

She left me an annuity for less than I had hoped, though it was generous, and also, in a touching failure of imagination, as if Dr. Grimstone could only envisage my future in my studio apartment in the Bronx (which she bought me twenty years ago when the building went co-op), sitting at that desk from her office, continuing my routine of those thirty-two years, she left me the desk and the stenographer's chair, along with the IBM Selectric typewriter, the adding machine, the plastic slipcovers for both, the heavy, gun-metal tape dispenser, and the tiny stapler, which, frankly, often jams.

The Madagascar Plan
of Julius Czaplinsky

EVERY FAMILY HAS its own myth of the lost fortune. The tragic plane crash that killed the oldest brother, whose wife and children are subsequently cut out of their rightful share in a family business. The missed opportunities to accept offers of partnership in endeavors that grew into Fortune 500 companies. If only grandfather had bought the waterfront acreage he was offered. If only grandmother had raised her paddle to buy the magnificent Picasso nude now hanging at The Art Institute of Chicago instead of the next lot, the smeary fake Chagall nude (on the facing page of that Parke-Bernet auction catalogue) now hanging over a cousin's fireplace. This chronicle, however, is not one of those stories of a tragic lost fortune. This is the story of a tragic found fortune.

In 1920, Eli and Morris Czaplinsky left their little brother Julius in Budapest with some cousins. There is no family lore, no details about what provisions, if any, they made for him. Did they feel guilty about Julius, abandoned at the last moment with the Fischer family, barely known second cousins on their mother's side? Or did they put him out of their minds completely as they sailed away, leaving him behind along with everything else that was familiar? He was fourteen years old; their parents had died just a few months earlier in an influenza epidemic (first one, then the other), and the brothers had promised their mother they would stay together. Now his two older brothers had foisted him on strangers who lived over a shop in a strange, bustling city, nothing like the small village, two day's walking distance from Budapest, where the Czaplinskys had been rooted for generations, proudly selling their live speckled chickens in the market square.

Did Eli and Morris miss him, as they began their new lives in America, peddling their candies from that unwieldy broken-down pushcart Eli found in an alley, that first pushcart that always smelled of fish no matter how much they scrubbed the splintery boards? Did they think of him and wonder how he was managing, as they boiled their sweets in the giant pot on the stove, as they wrapped the cooled barley sugar drops, as they ate their meals, as they tried to get used to the bland American flavors he might have enjoyed, or despised?

Did they wonder if that sour-looking Aunt Borbála ever give their little Julesy any sweet treats, a kiss goodnight, did she ever crack that *ferbissenah punim* to give him so much as a smile? Was he in school or had the Fischers put him straight to work in their dry goods business? Surely Eli and Morris had made promises to send for him when they could. Did they try to write to Julius, to Aunt Borbála? Did they think of sending money?

If Morris hadn't died in the 1921 diphtheria epidemic that swept New York, perhaps the brothers would have saved up enough money for his passage. What then? The joyful arrival of young Julius after those terrible but mercifully few years of separation, and after that, perhaps the three reunited brothers would have gone into business together. And who can say, Czaplinsky Brothers Candy might have been very successful, their sweets could have been delightfully appealing to young and old, and their business might have flourished, not only rivaling the likes of the now-vanished D. Auerbach & Sons, Peaks Mason Mints, or W. P. Chase in those halcyon years of candy manufacturing in New York City, but perhaps even outlasting them, swallowing them up, growing bigger and bigger. The synergistic energy of the three brothers might have made Czaplinsky a household name, maybe even the third big name in American candy, after Hershey and Mars, who can say?

But, of course, that never happened.

Here's what I imagine did happen. Yes, these are my perceptions. These are necessarily my interpretations of these events. Does anyone have a more authentic or plausible version of this story? If so, let's hear it!

Julius was grudgingly taken into the Fischer family, and as time passed he became more and more content with his life in Budapest, the so-called "Paris of the East," as his Aunt Borbála liked to say as she unfurled an array of the latest yard goods from France across the worn wooden counter of Fischer's on Dohány Street while persuading a prosperous customer that her social status required the more expensive Jacquard-loomed damask drapery materials favored in the most fashionable salons on *La Rive Droite*.

Julius finished school and went on to university, where he was a methodical but uninspired student, though he enjoyed the café life that surrounded the university. He wrote several letters to his brothers in America, but he could only address them to Morris and Eli Czaplinsky, care of General Delivery, New York City. He didn't know that Morris was dead or that Eli had moved to New Haven, Connecticut, where he had dropped the C and changed a letter and become a Ziplinsky. The name change made for simpler spelling and less confusion. Zip's Candies was such a good American brand name. And surely the change was also inspired by Eli's desire to make himself unfindable either by New York City detectives who could have wanted to discuss his presence at the Essex Market Courthouse the day Kid Dropper Kaplan was murdered, or by anyone nosing around on behalf of Little Augie, who surely wanted his money back, with interest.

Ziplinsky was anyway a little bit more of an American

kind of name than Czaplinsky, Eli thought, and it was a nice, zippy, peppy, zingy name at that. Changing it more would have signified shame about his heritage (he considered Zippel or Zipple but even with his beginner's English he recognized that would be undignified, too much like "nipple"). He looked down on all those Eastern European Jews who chopped their names the way generations of Czaplinskys whacked a cleaver through the necks of their squawking chickens, those Loewensteins who became Lows, a Rabinowitz now chopped to Robins, Borkowskys now answering to Bork. Then there were those Whites and Whitemans who were once Wiedermans, Grodners and Goldsteins who became Gordons. By the time Eli had become an American citizen in 1928, his proud signature was a boldly rendered E. Ziplinsky, with a big, flourishing Z, the bottom serif of the Z underlining the rest of the name, a habit he maintained to the end of his life.

Julius had no way of knowing that Eli had written to him five times from New York, the last time to tell him the sad news about their Morris having succumbed to diphtheria. The letters were intercepted by Aunt Borbála each time, who opened them when they arrived from America. Finding no money or specific promises about any, she hid the letters away in a desk drawer, feeling justified in keeping Julius from getting his hopes up. Maybe she would give him the letters some day, but not now. In the future, when he would thank her for keeping him grateful for what he had, for all that the Fischers had given him, instead of getting his hopes up dreaming about America. Julius was better off if he didn't think his brothers were going to send for him. These useless letters would keep him from forgetting his brothers. He needed to stop moping around so much, like he was always waiting for something.

If they did send money for Julius, she told herself, the first priority would be to pay her back for the expense and bother of having Julius added to her household. It was too bad about Morris, because now it was even less likely that any money would ever come. Eli was just a boy himself, and he would probably forget about Julius. Soon there were no more letters, which proved her right. Her father always said those Czaplinskys were good for nothing.

When Julius never heard from his brothers, he began to think they might both be dead, and even though Aunt Borbála never said anything, he tried on his own to make himself stop hoping for a letter. He didn't even know with any certainty that they had ever reached America. He continued to work behind the counter at Fischer's for several years until he left to go into business with his cousin Péter, the least gloomy and conceited of the Fischers, whose apprenticeship to an elderly baker in the old Jewish Quarter had given him skills and ambitions to open his own shop.

Fischer & Czaplinsky, a bakery with an adjoining coffee house on Kazinczy Street in the heart of the bustling Jewish Quarter (on the flat, Pest side of the Danube), thrived immediately, and within a couple of years there were five employees working alongside Julius and Péter to keep the customers satisfied with their good strong coffee and all their buttery little cookies and *kiffles*, *rigo jancsi*, flakey strudels, and especially their signature *kürtőskalácsok*, a yeasty sweet dough wound around cylinders that slowly rotated over hot coals until the pastry was browned.

Julius, now a handsome and prosperous citizen of the neighborhood, had become something of a ladies' man, with a series of girlfriends, each one believing that she would be the one to claim this attractive and slightly melancholy loner, that she would be the one with whom he would want to settle down and raise a family. But sooner or later, each one would discover evidence of a growing indifference combined with hints of a new woman in his life. Each one would withdraw, defeated, with a slightly broken heart, to be replaced by the next one, and the next.

Then Szilvia Weisz came to work in the bakery at Fischer
& Czaplinsky. She was a quiet little worker with a refulgent
smile and the nimblest fingers when it came to wrapping the
dough for the *kürtőskalácsok*, not too loose or it would fall onto
the coals, but not too tight or it would crack apart as it sizzled
and browned. Something shifted inside of Julius, some corner
of his brittle heart began to soften whenever he saw her, but
each time he asked her to go out with him, she refused, and
told him she would not go out with a playboy, no matter how
handsome or charming.

For six months she refused his advances until finally, when
he told her that he loved her and had not been with another
woman all that time (which was very nearly the truth), she
agreed to go to a chamber music concert with him, and then a
few nights later they went to dinner, and soon after that were
keeping company every evening, and then they were engaged
to be married, and then they were married, and the Weisz
family, all of them hardworking diamond buyers and cutters,
welcomed Julius, and made him feel truly part of a family
for the first time since he was a child. Soon there was a baby
girl, Matild, born in 1937, and after that a boy, Geza, born in
early 1939.

The First Jewish Law, restricting to twenty percent the
number of Jews who could have certain administrative positions or hold certain kinds of jobs, had been passed in 1938.
Ten years before that, the entire extended Fischer family
had converted en masse, and 27 of them all became church-
going Lutherans at once, and so they did not think these laws
applied to them. Two days after Geza was born, the Second
Jewish Law reduced the "economic participation" of the Jews
of Hungary to five percent, and soon after that the business
dropped the Czaplinsky name.

Cash payments to certain officials who were friendly with
other officials allowed the Fischer family to continue to avoid

being named as Jews. While Julius kept working on the bakery side, he was no longer welcome in any Fischer homes and he was asked to refrain from claiming any blood connection to them. Restoring his name to the business was nothing to discuss at this time, perhaps in the future, if peace should ever break out.

More and more Jews were moving from all over the countryside to Pest, and Fischer's had never been more filled with customers. Julius and Péter added as many more tables and chairs as they could cram in. Hungary's right-wing government was allied with Germany, and the quarter million Jews of Budapest, though more and more constricted by the new rules in their daily lives, continued to go to work, conduct their business, marry, have babies, and raise their families, believing that they were reasonably safe from further losses or restrictions. What more could happen?

Szilvia's younger sister Ágnes worked as a legal secretary for a prosperous law firm until she was forced to leave when the Second Jewish Law was passed. Her boss was quite sorry to lose such a pleasant and efficient worker. She was really an exceptionally beautiful girl, nice to look at every day, and she had such a good knowledge of German and French. He really regretted that she had to go, especially for such a shameful reason (he himself had a Jewish grandmother but thankfully nobody was aware of this blot on his record). When he encountered a government bureaucrat he had known since childhood, when they both went out to smoke cigars during an intermission at the opera, he put in a good word for Ágnes and all of her desirable attributes.

Ágnes, who was fortunately possessed of very fair, wispy hair and dark blue eyes, was soon offered employment in the Budapest central government offices as a correspondence typist-translator, where her German skills were desperately needed. The job was hers provided that she promised to keep her mouth shut about her background.

It was an open secret that the employment laws were enforced haphazardly, though the increasing power of the right-wing Arrow Cross Party was making both the Jews and their sympathizers more paranoiac with every passing day. Szilvia was home with the children and no longer worked at the bakery, but Julius would often come in the door at night with upsetting reports about groups of Arrow Cross Party members swaggering into the coffee house and forcing Jewish customers to vacate the tables they wanted. One afternoon Péter quietly took Julius aside to warn him that he might not be able to keep working at Fischer's much longer, and it might be safer for them all if he were to try and find something else, for now.

On a hot August night, Ágnes came for dinner with Szilvia and Julius, and after the babies were asleep, she took off her shoe and unfolded some sheets of onionskin paper, illicit extra carbon copies of documents she had translated into Hungarian and typed that afternoon. There was a memo from the Reich Central Security Office in Berlin titled *Reichssicherheitshauptamt: Madagaskar Projekt*. The author of the memo was Obersturmbannführer Adolph Eichmann.

The Madagaskar Projekt called for the resettlement of all the Jews of Europe on Madagascar, a million a year, over a period of four years. This was so much more desirable and efficient than the piecemeal efforts at deportation of Jews into centralized holding centers as they were flushed out from every city and every town and every village of Europe. No Jews, none at all, would remain in Europe.

The accompanying memo by Franz Rademacher, the recently appointed head of the *Judenreferat III der Abteilung Deutschland* (the Jewish Department of the Ministry of Foreign Affairs), which Agnes had also translated into Hungarian for distribution among the various government departments, included references to the stopping of construction of the Warsaw Ghetto and deportations of Jews into Poland, which had both been suspended on July 10th. *The Madagaskar Projekt* would render unnecessary all that effort to transport Jews into Poland for temporary containment.

The Madagaskar Projekt memo went on to detail issues of cost estimates for coordinating and commissioning sufficient fleets of seaworthy sailing vessels for the massive transportation effort that would be necessary, which depended largely on strategies for using ships from the British fleet, the imminent availability of which was confidently anticipated. The SS would carry on the Jewish expulsion in Europe, before ultimately governing the Jewish settlement.

Madagascar would only be a Mandate; the Jews living there would not be entitled to German citizenship. Meanwhile, the Jews deported to Madagascar would lose their various European citizenships from the date of deportation.

With all the Jews of Europe residents of the Mandate of Madagascar, this would prevent the possible establishment by Jews of a state of their own in Palestine. This would also help prevent any opportunity for them to exploit the symbolic importance of Jerusalem. The Madagascar Plan would create a central European bank funded with seized Jewish assets; this money would pay for the evacuation and resettlement of all the Jews, and it would also play a permanent role as the only permitted banking institution for any transaction between the Jews on Madagascar and the outside world. Herman Göring would oversee the administration of the Plan's economics.

Most significantly, the Jews remaining in German control on Madagascar would function as a useful bargaining chip for the future good behavior of the members of their race in America. The generosity shown by Germany in permitting cultural, economic, administrative and legal self-administration to the Jews on Madagascar would also be particularly useful for propaganda purposes. The administration and execution of the Madagascar Plan was assigned to various offices

within the Third Reich: Foreign Minister Joachim von Ribbentrop's office would negotiate the French peace treaty necessary to the handing over of Madagascar to Germany, and it
would also help design any other treaties required to deal with
Europe's Jews. The Information Department of the Foreign
Affairs Ministry, along with Josef Goebbels in the Propaganda Ministry, would filter all worldwide information about
the Plan. Viktor Brack of the Führer Chancellory would oversee transportation. There was no mention of any consideration
for the native population of Madagascar.

The three of them sat at the table studying the documents
until after midnight, talking very little. Finally, Julius crumpled together all the pages into a ball on a dinner plate and set
it alight with his cigarette.

Julius left for Madagascar three weeks later, the linings of
his coat and best three-piece suit filled with as many diamonds sewn in place as he could safely carry without attract-
ing attention. Péter had bought him out of the bakery and
coffee house with cash, less than Julius thought was fair, but
more than Péter had any obligation to provide, under the circumstances. Leaving only enough money for Szilvia to buy
what she and the babies would need for a few months, all the
rest of their savings had been converted to the highest grade
white diamonds, one and two carats each, thanks to Szilvia's
brother, who had a reliable and sympathetic source in Kim-
berley, South Africa. Julius had managed to get the highest
possible prices for Szilvia's beloved gray pearls, her grandfather's eighteen karat gold Patek Philippe pocket watch that
chimed on the quarter hour, and her great-aunt Lena's upright
piano, though the babies liked to hear Szilvia play it after dinner and Matild had cried when the men came to carry it down
the stairs.

Julius promised Szilvia he would get word to her as soon as
he could. He vowed that he would be sending for them just

as fast as possible, faster than she could imagine, they would all be together again, and safe once and for all. Although he could hardly bear to leave his family, he set out, determined to find a way to make a new and better life for Szilvia, Matild, and little Geza. Ágnes, too, and the rest of the Weisz family. And Péter, if he had the sense to raise his hand as a Jew and leave with his family, early instead of late, rather than live in fear of discovery all the rest of his days in Jew-cleansed Budapest.

Did those stuck-up Fischers think they wouldn't be found out? With those noses? How much praying on those sturdy Fischer knees in a fashionable Lutheran church would it take to change Aunt Borbála into a gentile from Buda instead of the imperious Jewess from Pest she had always been? Did they really believe they would be able to keep their place in the world that was changing around them?

Julius's arduous journey to Madagascar took almost six months. It had been surprisingly easy to get a visa for Zanzibar, with the assistance of Ágnes's supervisor, who gladly swapped a furtive and efficient groping from Ágnes for rubber-stamped traveling papers for Julius that would allow him to cross borders as he made his way south to the Greek coast. Julius took some trains, but mostly, he walked. From the Greek coast Julius sailed across to Egypt on a barge laden with barrels of olive oil. It was by then January of 1941. Working his way down the east coast of Africa, Julius arrived in Madagascar on a freighter from Zanzibar.

Okay, actually, I have no idea how Julius got from Budapest to Madagascar, or how long it took. His sons have told the story to their children over the years with too many and not enough explanations. I am the youngest of the five grandchildren of Julius Czaplinsky. This is how I am telling his story. And I confess to being at the limit of my imaginative ability for reconstruction of the most likely scenarios. Does it really matter? All of this happened, even if none of it's true. So let's just say that when we next see Julius, he has arrived in Madagascar from Zanzibar. It is the middle of March, the height of the hot rainy season. Picture him in your mind's eye. Have you got him? We pick up the narrative thread here:

The Malagasy dock workers think Julius Czaplinsky is a very funny sight indeed as he totters down the gangplank in his woolen three-piece suit, with his greatcoat folded over his arm, staggering slightly under the weight of his leather suitcase. As Julius traipses around the muddy, rutted lanes of the port town of Mahajanga, having spent most of the past month sweltering insanely in the heat so constantly that he thought he might die of heat suffocation, he finally feels that it would be safe enough to take off the jacket and vest of his suit with those precious diamonds sewn in the linings, and carry them over his arm with his overcoat. At last, he can wear his damp and grimy shirtsleeves rolled up to his elbows.

Julius has the Czaplinsky motivation and determination. He has arrived in Madagascar to figure out the best claim to stake, and then he plans to stake it hard and deep, ahead of the four million Jews who will soon begin to pour out of ships at every port, each of them hoping (as displaced Jews always do) to find a toehold to start a new life in this alien place.

Julius is here, you see, to get a jump on things, to get established ahead of all the competition. Should he buy buildings in towns, begin constructing simple housing on empty lots that he will be able to rent or sell at premium prices? Should he stake a strong position in shipping and import-export in one or more of the port towns? Should he buy arable land for agriculture? Where would it be most desirable for his family to live, in the central mountainous region or along one of the coasts? He has to find his way and think it all through, make the most of his advantage.

The Madagaskar Projekt had described the possibility of an all-Jewish administrative government that would be overseen by the SS. Perhaps he would qualify for consideration for some official position of authority, should that prove desirable, given his foresight about getting established early, without simply waiting to be one of four million souls rounded up and shipped to this strange island only 644 kilometers off the east coast of Africa, a world away from anything European Jews have ever known.

The Madagascar that Julius discovered was sparsely inhabited by a few Frenchmen here and there, but otherwise he was intrigued by the curious specimens of humanity he encountered everywhere he went. They didn't look like any people he had ever seen before in his life. The Malagasy people had probably never seen anyone who looked like him, either. Julius had the piercing blue Czaplinsky eyes and the familial beak of a nose (I have inherited both; I am unlucky that these features look better on the four grandsons, my brother and cousins, than on me, the lone granddaughter). He had a gaunt but nevertheless forceful bearing, though he couldn't have stood more than five foot eight. His wild hair was jet black, and it radiated out from his receding hairline, emphasizing his great domed forehead. Though clean-shaven in Budapest, Julius had sprouted a long dark beard by the time he arrived in Mahajanga on the Zanzibar ferry (or whatever).

His skin was of such a pale, pink, nearly alabaster hue that he burned terribly after even a few minutes in direct sun. In Madagascar, his face and neck burned repeatedly as the weeks passed, and darkened to a leathery brown, but Julius's body was otherwise still milky white, and any inadvertent exposure of his usually covered flesh was a fascination for the Malagasy who happened to catch such a glimpse. They called him *Vazaha*, white man, and wherever he went, they gathered to watch him eat, laughing with glee each time he pulled his spoon out of his pocket to eat his *Koba*, the pasty mash of rice, banana and peanuts that he had decided he could live on safely (after a few disastrous encounters with wretched, gristly bits of meat prepared with a stewy rice mixture studded with muddy bits of vegetation). As he fed himself this mash each day with his daintily deployed spoon, instead of scooping it from the bowl with his fingers the way everyone else did, he would remind himself from time to time, to make his meal more palatable, that he was the same man who had once sat in his high chair at the table with his family, being a good little boy, learning by example to spoon his mother's Sunday goulash from his bowl.

Julius was confident that he could figure out the best of his options, and he felt the urgency of his situation, but time seemed to tick by very, very slowly on Madagascar, and soon Julius fell into the rhythms of the island. He found a little hut where he could stay, in a crooked lane at the edge of Antanarivo where goats were tethered, and he paid some men to guard him while he slept, and to guard his things whenever he went out. The first nights, he was awakened continually by the sounds of geckos scrabbling across the earthen floor, and by the strange chirring sounds of the ring-tailed lemurs who swung from the trees and scampered about the underbrush with strangely graceful leaps, like a little troupe of two-toned, monkey-faced Cossacks.

Orb weaver spiders the size of grapefruits erected elaborate webs across his doorways while he slept, and he was unsettled each time he brushed into one of those webs inadvertently and made impact with the fuzzy scuttling body of its weaver. The hissing cockroaches startled him every time he disturbed one in the night when his bladder forced him to stir from his restless slumber. Julius was reluctant to leave his secret diamond hoard for more than short periods of time, and he knew he had to convert his stones to local currency, but the energies of living each day seemed to soak up all the hours of daylight and each crimson sunset found him hunkering down for the night once more with nothing accomplished.

Time passed.

He found a woman who would wash his clothes and prepare his food for him in a way that he could eat it. (It helped that she was very beautiful.) Mostly he lived on sweet potatoes, steamed manioc, and *mofo gasy*, a hearth-baked pancake made from sweetened rice flour. Night after night Julius dreamed of the sweet pastries he had served a thousand times in the coffee house, each one on a plate with the signature red and black striped rim incorporating the beautiful streamlined logo for Fischer & Czaplinsky, plates they continued to use even after the Czaplinsky name was scraped from the red, black and gold lettering on the windows and doors.

He dreamed of the unsold, stale pastries he had thrown away or given to beggars at the back door of the bakery at closing time night after night. *Kürtőskalácsok* unfurled in his dreams, flaky puffs of pastry unwinding from the baking cylinders, dropping in big, buttery curls that he couldn't quite catch before they blackened to ash on the glowing coals.

Months passed before Julius was able to make an approach to a French banker he had been observing in a cafe, a lonely alcoholic whose misbehavior involving certain accounting irregularities at his previous bank in Paris had led to his exile in this remote French colony. The banker was charmed by Julius, who had the prescience at their first meeting to make a gift of the small bottle of good Slivovitz he had tucked into his baggage and carried all this way and hoarded all this time.

Malagasy wine, which Julius had sampled, tasted like horse piss mixed with vinegar. Perhaps he should start a distillery. Did sufficient sugar cane grow on this or any other near enough soil? Would grapes on vines rot and mold in the humidity or would a vineyard be possible to contemplate establishing, perhaps on the windward side of the island? For modest kickbacks of which Julius was unaware, the banker made introductions for Julius to the right people who would give him the best prices converting his diamonds to Malagasy francs.

People are people, business is business, money is money. By the end of 1942, a land broker had secured Julius's rights to some four thousand hectares in the central rain forest region of the northern part of the island, in the Betsiboka region of the Mahajanga province, where the soil is rich and the humidity high. Half of his hilly lands were covered in a dense pine and eucalyptus forest, while the rest was a crazy quilt of 19th century French plantations fallen into disuse, though they had once yielded rich annual harvests of cacao, coffee, banana, and vanilla.

In Budapest, Julius had struggled to achieve and maintain a modest, bourgeois status. In Madagascar, where the Malagasy people lived a subsistence life on the land, his diamonds had bought such an unimaginable number of Malagasy francs that even after investing in these holdings, he was still an immensely rich man, with more houses than he could count scattered across his four thousand hectares, with dozens of overseers on his various lands, and hundreds of employees grateful for the very small wage he would pay them in exchange for working his plantations or providing whatever services he could possibly want or need. Time slowed and stopped. Time stood still for Julius.

By spring of 1943, Julius had become the monarch of a small kingdom. The rest of the world seemed extremely far away. His brilliant strategy had proven to be far more successful than he could have possibly imagined. He was the Founding Jew, the First Jew, the Only Jew of Madagascar! Julius was impatient for the first signs that the transports had begun. Each day he scanned the horizon. The unbroken sea was empty of ships, dotted only by a few of the small square-sailed primitive fishing vessels that went out early every morning to check their crayfish pots along the coastline. Surely, they would arrive today, or tomorrow?

Julius didn't consider that in faraway Budapest, time had not stood still. On Kazinczy Street, time had marched along quite briskly.

Every day Julius envisioned himself in his new role as the wise pioneer whose helpful advice would be eagerly sought by his people. He could see himself greeting and providing comfort and wisdom to as many of the newcomers as he could accommodate as they tumbled off the ships by the thousands, day after day, week after week, sailing into every port on the island, from Toliara to Antsiranana, each of them dazed, frightened, staggering under the weight of the few precious worldly goods they would have managed to bring along on the voyage from the Old World to this very New World.

We will begin again! Julius insisted to himself as he sipped the muddy coffee made from his own Caturra beans prepared for him each morning now by his house maid, and served to him on the verandah of his headquarters, a plantation house that overlooked five hundred acres planted in Trinitario and Criollo and Porcelana cacao. The openwork lace of the early morning mist floated through the tops of the banana canopy that soared over the hodge podge of the cacao trees. He longed for Szilvia, Matild, and Geza. And of course, Ágnes, too. He would welcome with open arms any of the Weisz family who wanted to come live on his plantations.

He was deeply moved by his own anticipated generosity as he envisaged himself presiding over his grateful family, perhaps dozens of them, all thankful that he had given them such a wonderful fresh start. He would be the patriarch, providing plenty for all. They would all be safe. They would all be prosperous. They would all be together again.

But the horizon remained empty. The ships filled with the Jews of Europe eager to begin their new lives did not arrive.

Julius had written to Szilvia steadily since his arrival, though the centralized postal service from Antanarivo was erratic at best and a complete disaster at worst, so he hadn't been overly worried to have not heard back from her in the beginning. But now when his letters continued to go unanswered, he had begun to fret. One morning as he sipped his coffee and gazed out over the treetops of his plantation it suddenly dawned on him with horror that while time stood still in Madagascar, it rushed ahead furiously and tumultuously and disastrously in the wider world.

That day he sent a long letter to the alcoholic banker in Antanarivo by messenger, with specific and urgent instructions for a wire to a correspondent bank in Budapest where the banker had told him long ago he might still have a contact who might be willing to deliver the message to Szilvia, or if that was risky, then to Péter, at the coffee house, who would surely be willing to pass a message to Szilvia. Wouldn't any banker in Budapest know Fischer's Bakery and Coffee House, on Kazinczy Street?

The wire Julius sent was three pages of dense advice about obtaining a visa for Zanzibar, traveling on the same route he had followed (whatever that was, let's agree that it's unimportant to the story), using the same sympathetic official as before, Ágnes's supervisor, the man who had approved his traveling documents. Julius's wire enumerated all the contact information he had for every leg of the journey, concluding with the name of the shipping clerk to see at the harbor in Stone Town once they arrived on Zanzibar.

The ensuing silence was ominous. Julius had heard nothing for too long. He felt a sudden spasm of terror, and with a sensation of horror he realized that he had been insanely complacent. Anything could have happened in all this time. He had to do something more, take some kind of action. He could no longer just sit and wait. He set out with one of his plantation managers in the most functional of his three rusting, patched-together Ford Model A trucks, but a summer monsoon had drenched the highlands for days, and after a day of fighting the mud that filled the narrow, winding track that led to his highland aerie, the truck was hopelessly mired, and they had only gone ten dozen kilometers. Julius had to make the journey to Antanarivo in the back of a zebu cart. The jolting, slow-motion trip took many days, and he arrived feeling quite sick from the rocking of the cart and from the fear that now clutched his heart. How could he have been so blithely unconcerned all these months, months which had turned to years? It was now July of 1944.

The dissipated and habitually hung-over banker arranged for Julius to use one of the few telephones on Madagascar that could connect him to Budapest, in the central government office across from the bank. Julius had developed a fluent Malagasy-inflected French, and he was able to make his needs understood well enough. It took nearly an hour to make the connection, but finally, miraculously, the series of necessary operators were able to hold all the necessary connections to patch through to Budapest.

He gave the number to the local operator there in Hungarian, his eyes filling with tears as he spoke the familiar numbers in Hungarian to another Hungarian speaker, but a moment later her faint voice in his ear told him through the echoing static that the number was no longer in service.

Ah, of course, Szilvia was economizing. He begged the operators not to disconnect the line and then he gave the next number that came into his head, for Fischer & Czaplinsky, now Fischer's Bakery and Coffee House. Surely Péter would be willing to relay his message to Szilvia. The call went through more quickly this time, and he could hear the familiar ringing tones echoing faintly down the line.

"Bitte?"

An unfamiliar voice, with the clatter of the coffee house in the background. Why answer the phone at Fischer's in German? A wrong number? A bad joke? Julius's mind was racing in slow motion, every thought slippery and ungraspable. In carefully enunciated Hungarian he asked if this was Fischer's and the man said, "Ja, ja," impatiently, before demanding, "Wen wollen Sie sprechen? Was wollen Sie?"

Julius switched to his rudimentary German and asked for Péter. The German laughed, a short mirthless bark, and said Péter had gone for a little swim in the Danube, and then he hung up.

Julius didn't know that even while he was still making his way towards Madagascar, the transports of Jews from German territories into occupied Poland had resumed, as had work to complete the fortifications of the Warsaw Ghetto. Eichmann's beloved *Madagaskar Projekt* had stalled. Germany had not achieved a quick victory over Britain (the Battle of Britain had not gone as predicted so confidently by the Luftwaffe, despite their colorful maps and pins), and so the British fleet, crucial to the *Madagaskar Projekt*, would not be available to ship all the Jews to their island colony in the Indian Ocean after all. There was no alternative means of efficiently transporting four million Jews out of Europe.

In late August 1940, Rademacher begged Ribbentrop to hold a meeting at his Ministry so they could revise the *Madagaskar Projekt* and put it in motion. Ribbentrop did nothing. Eichmann's Madagascar memo was never approved by Heydrich's office. From time to time, one or another official of the Third Reich would raise the question of a future plan for the ghetto colony on Madagascar for all the Jews of Europe, but by early December of that year, it had been abandoned entirely. The *Madagaskar Projekt* was stillborn, and the massive logistical quagmire of Jewish deportations would be solved another, more efficient way. If the Jewish island colony in the Indian Ocean was a First Solution, then the answer to the vexing Jewish Question would be the Final Solution.

I have to admit the timeline is way off here. Why is the sudden and successful British invasion of Madagascar in May of 1942 not in this story? I suppose it's not really credible that Julius had no awareness of the stealth landing in Courrier Bay by the combined forces of the 13th Assault Flotilla. He had already been on Madagascar for more than a year at that point. So let's allow for the possibility that he welcomed the British forces. Perhaps he even played a small role, and had a secret involvement in the mysteriously deployed guiding beacons that enabled the invading, unlit British flotilla to glide past the dangers in the shoals of the harbor and land the troops safely in the darkness, while the Vichy slept. That would be good, if Julius did that. It improves the story. It's good for the family. Let's say he did these things.

Soon after the British had secured Madagascar, Free French forces took over from the Vichy government. But looking at Julius's land acquisitions, I have to admit that a less nice version of this narrative has Julius doing business with the Vichy officials one way or another from the moment he arrives on the island in March of 1941. The drunken banker is thick as thieves with them. The Vichy haven't got much to do, governing this godforsaken jungle in the middle of the Indian Ocean, and Julius is an amusement. They are willing to assist this pushy, ambitious Hungarian Jew with his coat full of diamonds in securing a position of power and authority in advance of the hordes. Why not? He will be useful to them.

Perhaps Julius is unhappy to see the corrupt Vichy officials replaced by the Free French officers who now govern the island, as it dawns on him that the chances of the Madagascar Projekt being executed as proposed are dwindling with every passing day. Surely the Third Reich wouldn't want to go to the trouble and expense of delivering the Jews of Europe to Madagascar, only to see them pick up and take themselves wherever in the world they pleased after that. Even without knowledge of what has transpired in Europe, it is clear that without the Vichy in control of Madagascar, the plan collapses.

Perhaps Julius recognized then that he and he alone has escaped to Madagascar, while his family, everyone he has left behind, will be swallowed up by the incoming tide of history. Perhaps he never tried to reach them at all. Perhaps he did nothing but cultivate his holdings and wait. He is helpless. What can he do, from here, but hope for the best?

It is established fact that Julius Czaplinsky spent the war years on Madagascar, where he was both safe and extraordinarily prosperous. But he died there, too, of malaria, soon after the end of the war, at the age of forty-two. Julius left behind his beautiful, young common-law wife, called Lalao (she had been his housekeeper), and their two children, Darwin, who was two, and Huxley (my father), who was an infant when Julius died.

I don't really have a good way of telling this story seamlessly. While it is true that it is somewhere between difficult and impossible to reconcile the timeline completely, or really nail down the facts one way or the other, how important is that in the larger scheme of things? Is any family story ever completely accurate? Can we just skip over these discrepancies? Julius was isolated on Madagascar, from the moment he arrived, and so in a way he was a prisoner of his circumstances. The larger truths of this story are what matters, and it would be pointless to get too distracted by these details. In fact, a failure of imagination may be the most honorable choice here. Think of it this way: If for even a brief moment any of us could possess the full realization of all the horrors of human experience, how would it be possible to live?

Julius had no way of knowing that Germany had occupied Hungary in 1944, when Hungary was on the verge of negotiating with the Allies after the German losses on the Eastern front. Nor did he know that tens of thousands of Hungarian Jews had already been killed in labor camps and deportations even before the occupation.

He would not have been able to imagine that the shul on Dohány Street had been turned into a small concentration camp. Adolf Eichmann himself had taken over the rabbi's office behind the beautiful rose window in the women's balcony. Eichmann organized a Budapest Jewish council to oversee the Jews who remained in Hungary, all 200,000 of them, now concentrated in Budapest, crammed into 2,000 homes scattered through the city, each designated Jewish dwelling marked with a conspicuous yellow Star of David.

Julius did not know that nineteen people had been assigned to his apartment, and that for several miserable months Szilvia, Matild and Geza had shared a narrow bed in what had been Matild's room, a room in which four strangers also slept.

Nor did he know that The Arrow Cross party members had rampaged through the Jewish Quarter, shooting hundreds of Jews and throwing their bodies into the Danube, Péter among them. Szilvia, Matild and Geza (my aunt and uncle who never grew up!) were among the thousand dead Hungarian Jews who lay buried in the mass graves in the courtyard of the synagogue on Dohány Street, just up the street from where Fischer's dry goods shop once did business, before the Arrow Cross burned it to the ground with seven members of the Fischer family, who had refused to wear their yellow stars, locked inside.

What of Ágnes, the bearer of the smuggled secret *Madagaskar Projekt* document that sent Julius on his odyssey from Budapest to an unimaginable island in the Indian Ocean east of Africa? She had been arrested and placed in the Kistarcsa transit camp for two months before she was marched with hundreds of other prisoners all the way to the Austrian border in freezing November sleet. On the third day of the march, so weakened by a fever that she was unable to walk, Ágnes was shot and killed with a single bullet to her head. Her body was last seen by other prisoners as they marched past where she lay at the side of the road.

By the end of 1944, here is what Julius Czaplinsky did know. He was thirty-eight years old. His wife and children were dead. He was rich beyond imagining. He was safe from the turmoil of war. And he was utterly alone. The other four million Jews of Europe weren't coming. There would never be one ship unloading its bewildered cargo of Jews, let alone a fleet of ships, a legion of Jews arriving to establish anew, to begin again. There would never be a single grateful recipient of all the wisdom and generosity Julius was so prepared to bestow upon his *landsmen*. The *Madagaskar Projekt* had brought only Julius Czaplinsky, the first, last, and only Jew on Madagascar.

Diamond District

"LET THE STONE TELL YOU what it wants to be and allow it to become that thing," the old man whispered. Sarah peered through the loupe and bent over her grandfather's worktable. She gazed intently at the diamond he was showing her.

"You see?" he commanded. "Study it well. Do you remember how it looked when I showed it to you last week and told you this one I would next be cutting?"

"A white pebble, a lump of salt?" Sarah had been tempted to taste it, but at ten, she knew better. She gave him back the loupe. She spent every afternoon after school in her grandfather's little workspace on 47th Street, way in the back of the third floor in one of the oldest buildings in the diamond district, while her mother gave piano lessons on the Bosendorfer in the apartment. The three of them lived together on West 76th Street, over a well-known funeral parlor.

Sarah watched her grandfather work at his bench, knowing that he mustn't be disturbed unless he spoke to her first, knowing that his work was as delicate as brain surgery. She had been doing her history homework in the dim light of a stubby gooseneck lamp at his old cluttered desk where his paperwork was stacked, waiting for the moment when her grandfather would stand up, take off his special magnifying headpiece with its lighted lens, stretch, turn off his work light, slowly stow his tools, and then lock the tray of stones away in the clanking safe bolted to the floor under his workbench.

"Yes, that's right," he answered finally, after a pause so long she had turned back to the Battle of Gettysburg. "Like something unimportant you might bring home from the seashore. But its beauty was hidden. And now what do you see? It is revealed." He spoke softly without looking up, as if he were talking to himself. "This is called an emerald cut. If you can let the properties of the diamond guide you, then you will have something wonderful. If you try to force it to be something it doesn't want to be—pffft! It could shatter. Or it could resist you in a thousand other ways I will explain to you someday. Just remember that if you are wrong in your choice, then the stone will sulk and refuse to be what you want, because you are mistaken about its true nature. Then you have nothing."

Walking to the subway, they passed brightly lit shop windows, one after the other, displaying nothing but bare blue velvet landscapes, empty red velvet stages, barren black velvet amphitheaters. Sometimes, on days they left a little early, Sarah would see hands reaching, reaching, reaching into the windows, taking away the precious merchandise to be locked up safely until the next day of business. She reached for her grandfather's hand, and the rough calluses on his palm were like precious pebbles they carried home together.

Thistles

"I LOVE PEOPLE more than anything."

Natalie Oliver looked up from her book at the woman who had broken the silence. There were nine of them still waiting in the jury room for voir dire questioning, seated around the big table as if they were expecting a meal to be served. The jury room was somehow both chilly and stuffy; condensation misted the smeary unopenable window. The repetitively-discussed cold snap seemed to guarantee a white Christmas just three days away. If they were chosen for this jury, the trial wouldn't start until early January, they had been told by the court officer who had called out their dozen names and led them to a courtroom, where they had sat in the jury box and listened to presentations by both sides of the case.

Street noise and the faint clanging bell of a scrawny Salvation Army Santa in front of the courthouse steps punctuated the quiet in the jury room. A limp swag of silver tinsel taped haphazardly around the door further signified the season. Natalie could envision the succession of Valentine hearts, four-leaf clovers, Easter eggs, American flags, and Thanksgiving turkeys that would similarly enhance the room's ambience throughout the year.

The people-lover plucked at the tattered magazines that lay in a heap in the middle of the table that took up most of the room. Nobody else had touched them. Two people were sitting with their eyes closed, like tired commuters. One woman had put her head down on her folded arms and appeared to be sleeping. Everyone else was gazing down at a phone. Natalie was the only person on this jury panel with a book.

"I love people," she repeated. Natalie wasn't certain if the woman was trying to chat philosophically with anyone up for it about her fondness for humanity or her preference for a magazine. Natalie nodded politely, though she hadn't been addressed particularly. "My late husband liked *Popular Mechanics* the best," the talker added. Okay, *People*, then.

A tall thin man, who Natalie had noted was wearing a sufficient number of shirts over shirts to qualify as an architect, raised his eyebrows and glanced their way as he continued to pore over personal advertisements in the local counterculture weekly that he had pulled out of his battered messenger bag. He didn't seem like an "Other News" reader. Maybe he was checking the local live music schedule. Or the snarky restaurant reviews. She thought he had an intriguing, melancholy look to him.

He caught Natalie's eye, and they grinned at each other for a moment. Oh, hello. Even when he smiled, something in his face stayed serious, she thought. She could feel his gaze lingering as she looked away.

Natalie fidgeted in her seat, unused to having to organize her legs in tights and a skirt. *Jurors are expected to dress in a manner reflective of the formality of the court proceedings.* A jewelry designer and silversmith, she worked alone in her New Haven studio on commission, mostly for New York stores, and at times she went for months without putting on a skirt or dress.

An exceptionally successful new group of carved jade-and-amethyst link bracelets had kept her frantic since September with Christmas orders from her one local seller, an excellent jewelry store on Chapel Street that always gave her a corner of their window display, but those had all been delivered last week. She had been commissioned by a grateful patient to make rose gold cufflinks in the shape of a patella for an orthopedic surgeon, and those, she was told, had been well-received. The last work was on three nearly-finished pairs of asymmetrical cluster earrings promised by the end of the week to the store—these featured a variety of small, low-grade cushion-cut pink and emerald-cut yellow diamonds, stones Natalie had discovered a few years before, quite by accident, while picking up an order of little rough-cut emeralds and rubies from her gem dealer in the back of the largest Diamond District arcade on 47th Street in New York.

Looking for the stones he had set aside for her, the elderly diamond merchant (he had told her once that his hands were no longer steady enough for cutting stones, though he was once known for his talents, so now he only bought and sold) had pulled out the wrong black velvet-lined drawer from his case. When he emptied one of the thick white paper envelopes from the drawer onto the counter tray, she was intrigued by the quick glimpse before he swept them back into the unfolded packet with a practiced hand, muttering to himself about the foolish brifka error. She asked him to empty that one again so she could see these diamonds. He shrugged and obliged her. She traced a fingertip through the swale of assorted diamonds, which were a variety of colors and sizes and cuts, none more than a half carat, some of them tiny, which the dealer dismissed as "low quality strops, just crumbs, a melee—we only sell as a bundle, you can't choose."

Odd little diamonds like these—unmatchable, clouded with inclusions, the smallest of them only single cut—are considered inferior, undesirable, and not really worth anyone's time. Yet all the dealers had a drawer or two of stones like these, even if nobody wanted to sell them and nobody wanted to buy them. And someone, somewhere (probably India or China), had cut and polished each one of them. The larger stones were even full cut. The pale greens and pinks and yellows charmed

Natalie inexplicably. All the hours spent, all the hands these inconsequential diamonds had passed through on their way to being merchandise, castoff crumbs indeed, compared to the highest-grade stones bought and sold here every day.

Natalie had never particularly liked ordinary diamonds, the ones valued by most people for their clarity and brilliance, and she never worked with them, not only because of price. She thought diamonds were boring. But she was drawn to the subtleties of these unloved little gems, which at first glance most people would probably assume to be citrine, or pink tourmaline. While she sifted through them, the dealer muttered impatiently in Yiddish and then echoed in English— why bother with these useless, left-footed boots for which I give you a good price?

Sold! she had replied. Now she used these odd, tiny, multicolored diamonds all the time, and they had become something of a signature in her work, played cunningly against larger opaque stones like chrysoprase, or agate, or lapis lazuli. She had resisted the temptation to raise her prices, even though she knew she could. People willingly pay more for anything identified as a diamond.

Once she gave these earrings (each pair was set with the same combination of stones but in a different pattern) a little final finishing and added her tiny maker's mark, Natalie's season was over, and in the quiet of her studio she had felt so isolated that she had begun to work on some onyx-and-silver cuff links that she sort of thought she maybe might send to her ex-boyfriend Mark for Christmas, though she doubted he would think to send her a present.

They had gone out for three years, and the break-up at the end of the summer had come to feel like the obvious end point for both of them. Natalie knew from his Facebook page that he was seeing someone new, a presumably divorced or separated graduate student with a young child and better privacy settings than Mark's. Maybe that was why she hadn't quite finished the cuff links and probably wouldn't. His drawer of dress shirts with French cuffs now seemed like an affectation.

The architect-looking guy drummed his fingers in an impatient rhythm on the table. Natalie looked down at her own hands. She rarely wore rings. Bare of any jewelry, they looked capable, but also lonely and plain.

In these recent darkening days leading to Christmas, whenever she tried to make plans with nearby friends, every single one of them seemed to be in the throes of some terrific new romance, paired off with some wonderful, exciting man or woman, committed to this or that holiday party or performance. Their Facebook pages had become unbearable. Any time she went on Facebook she was reminded all over again why she should never go on Facebook. She usually felt in the swim of things, but right now Natalie couldn't remember when she had ever spent so much time this left out, this alone. Certainly not since junior high school. When the summons for jury duty had appeared in her mailbox, it had felt almost like an invitation. Getting dressed this morning, Natalie could only hope that wanting to serve on a jury didn't automatically disqualify you.

She had read it through so many times she had begun to perseverate the words of "Your Guide to Jury Duty." *Use discretion in selecting your attire. Decorum is maintained in the courtroom; please dress accordingly.* Like Miss Peavey's painfully proper ballroom dancing classes, in other words, minus the white gloves.

Natalie's old corduroy skirt and a Guatemalan cardigan sweater had seemed exactly right when she put them on, but now she felt dowdy and trapped by the thick material and scratchy wool, not herself. On an average solitary day in the studio Natalie wore leggings or jeans with plain black turtlenecks, because in the course of the day she would wear several different pieces of her own jewelry, forever testing out weight, balance, stone settings, clasp hardware, comfort. Today she had selected an experimental pendant in the shape of a patella, on an open-looped chain of small hammered circles, a prototype for a new design.

The architect was staring at her again—no, he was looking at her breasts—or maybe he was scrutinizing her necklace. Natalie tried to intercept his gaze, expecting a sheepish or embarrassed look, but he seemed so intent on whatever part of her he was studying that he remained oblivious to her counter-stare. Natalie realized the attention felt good even though it was verging on too much.

The door to the jury room opened, and the court officer stuck his head in and beamed at the remaining members of the jury pool as if they were exceptionally cooperative kindergarteners, as he had done each time he came for the next prospective juror for voir dire.

"Three down, nine to go," he said, his eyes roving around the table, counting them. Natalie looked around the room too, imagining the disparate group of characters in a B movie about shipwrecked castaways in a lifeboat.

The architect guy could be the captain—noble, dedicated, but harboring some sad secret. Maybe she could be the lonely socialite escaping her past. Though from different walks of life, though doomed to die here beyond hope of rescue, they were meant for each other.

The court officer (the loyal bosun?) squinted at the document in his hand and called out, "Jablonski, Angela."

A skinny woman with tattooed eyebrows (murderess on the lam), whose poorly-cast chunky gold topaz ring—it had an uneven bezel—had caught Natalie's eye, pushed back from the table and stood up, scowling, before sauntering after him. Nothing discreet or decorous about that one, thought Natalie, eyeing her short, off-clean down vest with fur trim. A walking peremptory challenge. The door banged shut behind her.

"We having fun yet?" muttered the small man across the table (the mutinous first mate), who sported a creepy little rat's tail of bleached hair curling down behind the collar of his jacket. He leaned back in his chair and pretended to yawn. Natalie could feel him trying to attract her attention. The woman who loved *People* (helpless diamond-encrusted dowager) yawned too.

Under his short denim jacket, the first mate's T-shirt bulged and rippled as he stretched his arms over his head in a practiced gesture that Natalie thought was calculated to show off his pecs, delts, lats, tris, bis, abs, and whatever else he had developed under there. The captain grinned at her again, and their eyes met in a moment of conspiratorial amusement.

"Lunchtime, people," the bailiff said, sticking his head in the door. That was quick. The murderess must have been dismissed. "Wear your juror buttons. No discussing the case. Avoid anyone from either table in the courtroom if you see them on the street or in the elevator. Be back here by two. You're getting more than an hour, folks."

Out on the blustery street in front of the courthouse, Natalie stood for a moment, clearing her head, trying to decide if she wanted to skip lunch and use the time to walk to her studio and catch up on some paperwork. It was only a few blocks away, but how much could she get done, really, given that walking there and back would use half the lunch break?

"A Natalie Oliver, isn't it?"

It was the putative architect/captain. He nodded and looked directly at Natalie's hands where she was buttoning her coat. She drew a blank, followed his gaze, and then got it. Her pendant.

"Oh, this," she said, fingering the lightly-dimpled silver disc. "Yes, as a matter of fact it is a Natalie Oliver. How did you recognize it?"

"I know her work—it's terrific. I've never seen a piece like this one, but I've been looking at it all morning, and it just has that sensibility. May I?"

Natalie smiled and said nothing as he took the pendant from her fingers and turned it over in the palm of his glove. The length of the chain required that they stand much closer than the ordinary street-corner conversational distance between strangers. He looked puzzled.

"That's odd," he murmured.

"What's odd?" Natalie studied his face. In the courthouse she had put him in his forties, but up close in the daylight she realized he had dark circles under his eyes that aged him; he was probably in his thirties, like her.

"No maker's mark. She always signs her pieces with a little sort of chop mark, an N inside an O. It's not here, though." He took off a glove and rubbed the blank back of the pendant with his thumb, as if he could detect the mark that way.

"It's not signed—this piece isn't finished. Hey—we haven't really met, you know." Natalie looked up again into his rather sad-looking brown eyes. She put out her hand. "Natalie Oliver, actually."

He let go of the pendant and looked up to meet her gaze, stepping back to more ordinary speaking distance between strangers on a street corner. He took off his other glove to take her outstretched hand. "Oh, gosh. You must think I'm an idiot. Peter. Peter Lewis. An idiot who admires your work named Peter Lewis. Your hand is cold," he added with some concern, holding it for a moment between both of his. "I've kept you standing on the windiest corner in New Haven. Hey—you want to get some lunch? Do you know this neighborhood?"

They went up the street to an old-fashioned coffee shop that Natalie frequented regularly for several reasons: It was quick, cheap, and she loved the listing on the menu for "plate of ice cream." She always had a grilled cheese with tomato. Also, the place reminded her of the Edward Hopper painting *Nighthawks*. The waitresses, sisters, always made Natalie feel she belonged. Peter had never been in Whitney Dairy before, but Sheila called him sweetheart and Kitty told him he ought to have a bowl, not a cup, of lentil soup with his grilled cheese, because he was too thin, and baby it's cold outside. As she collected their menus, she informed them that they were ordering a plate of fries, for the table, and they didn't argue.

"So, it's not a murder trial, but don't you think the roofing contractor kind of looks like a hit man?" Natalie asked cheerfully after Kitty had headed to the back to shout their order into the kitchen through the hatch. The case for which they were empaneled was boringly civil, not criminal—a dispute about a leaky shopping center roof.

"We can't discuss the case!" Peter looked around in mock alarm as if to see if her intemperate remark had been overheard by any courtroom personnel.

"Oh, okay. Sorry, sorry." True enough. They had been admonished not to discuss the case. She tried to think of a different subject. "Voir dire, funny how American legal procedures are full of Latin and French terms."

"True dat," said Peter. "You know, the literal meaning of voir dire. Speak true. Say the truth. True dat."

On the walk up Whitney Avenue to lunch, she had learned that Peter was a graphic designer, not an architect, but he worked for a large architecture firm, doing all its graphics and signage, so she had been nearly right. He lived in a converted boathouse on the water out past Long Wharf, in a neighborhood Natalie hadn't known existed. When a slow-moving fire truck passed them, Peter had saluted the driver, who had saluted back. He still knew a lot of the hook and ladder guys, he explained, because his father was a retired firefighter with the East Battalion. Natalie didn't know the Fire Department had battalions.

"Battalion sounds French."

"French from the Italian from the Latin," Peter agreed.

"So have you ever actually answered a personal ad?" Natalie blurted after a moment's silence, after they had ordered. "You were reading the personal ads in the back of 'Other News' so intently, that's why I'm asking. Maybe you were studying the typography and the layout. I mean, you don't seem like someone who would. Answer one. I mean, I wouldn't. But I love to read them, too. There's something quaint about personal ads in the back of a weekly counterculture newspaper instead of online. Missed Connections are my favorite. Help. I'm babbling." Peter's bark of laughter provided a graceful stopping point for Natalie's chatter.

"I'm not laughing at you. It's just the way you remind me of someone, the way your train of associations gets rolling," he said after a moment. "Anyway, believe it or not, I placed one of those 'Other News' ads—that's what I was looking at—but it's not for me, it's for Gus, my father."

"Do you know someone for my dad?" Natalie quoted. "I *noticed* that one in this week's ads. Really. Listen: 'Likes to cook, fixes things that aren't broken, talks back to six o'clock news.'"

"You really do scrutinize those personal ads," Peter said.

"Not usually. Actually, I was thinking of answering the ad," Natalie replied, a little defensively.

"He's not your type. Way too old. Too grumpy. You can do better."

"You don't know what my type is."

Sheila brought their food and they began to eat.

"Seriously, I was thinking of my mother," Natalie continued. "She lives in a condo in Northbury near the water. She hates to cook, breaks things, and talks right through the six o'clock news."

Peter eyed her. "Seriously?"

"Yes. Lillian's sixty-two. My father died six years ago. I really am serious. But she's difficult. Not the most easygoing is putting it politely. We don't get along very well. Or we do, as long as we don't spend much time together. Then we get along terrifically. But tell me about Gus. Your ad said he's seventy, right?"

"Right, just last month, actually. My sister flew in from Colorado and we threw him a party with a lot of his Central Station buddies, but he ended up doing most of the cooking. Mom died when I was a senior in high school, and then Gus had this girlfriend for about ten years, the widow of an Engine Four guy, actually. Martha was okay, but then she got cancer and died. That was a couple of years ago." Peter dipped the last of their shared French fries into the puddle of ketchup on the edge of his side of the plate and ate them absentmindedly.

"So how do we do this?" Natalie signaled Kitty for more coffee. Kitty gave her a secret little pat of approval on the shoulder as she refilled their mugs and cleared empty plates.

"I hadn't really thought that through," Peter said, stirring a tiny amount of sugar into his mug with precision. "I just figured I would cook up some way to introduce him if the right person answered the ad."

"Say I answered it," Natalie said. "I mean, now what? I think maybe I ought to meet Gus first, to see if it even makes sense. But I'm sure Lillian would never be willing to meet someone this way."

"They have that in common, at least. The thing is, he really likes women, and he hates being alone. I keep having this fear that he'll be scooped up by someone who isn't good enough, that he'll settle for the next nice lady who comes along, for the company. But Gus would hate the ad, you know—the idea of the ad. I figured I would make up something plausible if anyone answered."

"You mean like, 'Hi Dad, I want you to meet your new girlfriend who I just happen to know from yoga class?'"

"I think I can do better than that."

"Has anyone answered?"

"Only you."

Kitty brought their checks, which they paid separately, and they headed back to the courthouse.

"So, are you interested in jewelry design?" Natalie asked, aware that she was walking a little more slowly than her usual brisk pace, though their time was nearly up. "You seem so observant of every tiny detail, which is pretty unusual for a man."

"Shockingly sexist remark," Peter rebuked, but his tone was playful.

"You're right. But seriously—do you mentally redesign everything you see?"

"Not *everything*," Peter said, giving her a sidelong look.

"Shockingly sexist remark," Natalie said as they continued down the street. They laughed together, both a little self-conscious. "But really," Natalie persisted, "Have you ever designed jewelry? You have the sensibility for it."

"No, I don't know much about jewelry making. It interests me—I'd love to watch you work sometime. But it's strictly aesthetics for me, not the science of it, the metalwork, hardening and annealing and all that."

"Sounds like you do know about the science of it."

"Only a little bit, theoretically. I really like your work. It's always so balanced and surprising and inevitable. I'm glad Fred Wilton always has a few of your pieces."

"Thank you. Seriously."

"And I do have a strong association that means a lot to me. There used to be someone in my life who loved your stuff. She had several pairs of your earrings, you know the chased vermeil circles? And a pin, one of the ones you did a few years ago, with a swirl of cabochon jade ovals around that little pink diamond . . ." Peter trailed off, looking pensive.

"Who was she to you?" Natalie asked, resisting the urge to put her hand on his arm. (She also resisted the urge to correct him needlessly—what he called jade was actually chrysoprase.) He looked sad again. They walked a block before he answered. Natalie was beginning to wonder if he was going to say anything at all or just ignore the question, which now felt like one she shouldn't have asked.

"Look, I really didn't mean to tell you about this here and now," Peter said. "I'm going to tell you, because it's come up, but I don't want you to feel that you have to react in any particular way, okay? In fact, it would suit me if you don't react at all."

"Okay." Natalie waited.

Peter took a deep breath and let it out. He kept his eyes focused on some middle distance.

"She was my wife. Sarah. She died last year of metastatic breast cancer. She was a cellist—we met because she was at the Yale School of Music, and my firm was just at the end of the big renovation of Stoeckl Hall. She taught cello to kids after school as a side gig, and she came storming into our office because the practice room floors were closed while we installed all the signage and painted all the room markers. Someone in her department had promised her access to her practice room by that date on the calendar, when it was months away, and now, with some delays, the work wasn't complete, and it was impossible, and dangerous, with those toxic solvents, for anyone to get inside the building. But that promise was a fortunate mistake that changed my life, and hers.

"Sarah had looked up the address of our firm, and then she marched straight across the Green and down Chapel Street all the way to our office, which is quite a hike, the other side of the tracks, literally, past Wooster Square, and she had stormed right in to tell us how we had ruined her week and cost her money and she might lose some students and blah blah blah. I was in charge of the signage, so everyone else hid and I was sent out front to deal with her.

"My office couldn't believe I was going out with Crazy Cello Lady when they found out. That was six years ago—we got married after we had been together a year. So that's why I know your beautiful jewelry so well. She loved it. And the last year of her life was ghastly, nothing stopped the cancer, which was in her liver, and then her brain, and then her bones, and she suffered horribly, and I've been in hell, and now we're going back to that small, airless room with those other weird people and we're not going to talk about it anymore. Okay?"

Natalie took his arm and stopped him. They were at the courthouse. She forced down the waves of sympathy that had been rising inside her and tried to distance herself for a moment. Several other people from their jury pool were going up the steps, including the rich dowager and the mutinous first mate, together, deep in animated conversation.

"Okay," she said, trying to speak neutrally. "But Peter—"

"Yes?"

"I do want to meet Gus."

They were back out on the courthouse steps only ten minutes later. The suit had been settled during the break.

"Merry and happy, folks, as the case may be," the court officer had said when he dismissed them. "Your civic duty has been rendered. Connecticut jury law—one day, or one trial. All done."

Natalie and Peter had ducked into the same elevator moments later, having concluded simultaneously that they didn't want to participate in the dowager's stated plan to swap names and addresses all around.

"I think she's planning annual reunions," Peter said. "It's been such a fabulous experience. I think our group really bonded. I can't wait to mark my calendar."

"What's good for you? How about never? Is never good for you? It works for me," Natalie quipped awkwardly. That was lame. And the opposite of what she hoped would come next. If it weren't for Peter, she would have been disappointed that she wouldn't serve on a jury and go through a trial.

They stood together on the steps again. The moment length-
ened.

"I should get back to the office, I guess," Peter finally said.
"So, look. Gus. Do you really want to check him out for your
mother, seriously? I'm supposed to go there for dinner tomorrow night. Why don't I bring you along? Would that be okay?"

"Yes. Whatever. Yes," Natalie said. "But what's the cover
story? What are you going to tell him about me?"

"I'll tell him you're this really interesting woman I met on
jury duty, if that's all right with you. The fewer tangled webs,
the better, you know? Anyway," Peter said, reaching out with
his index finger to gently touch the surface of Natalie's pendant for a moment, "it's true."

Gus lived on a winding Hamden street Natalie knew from
her marathon training phase a while back, when she routinely
ran a six-mile loop through New Haven and Hamden. She
had always thought of it as the *Leave It to Beaver* neighborhood, and she had liked this street particularly, as much for
its friendly porches and lawns as for its absence of menac-
ing dogs. Turning the familiar curves and corners in Peter's
ancient Volvo, Natalie realized she hadn't been out this far in
more than a year—Mark wasn't a runner and he had resented
the time her runs took out of a Saturday, and since the break-
up she hadn't returned to her running routine with the same
commitment—and she resolved to extend her thrice-weekly
short runs in order to get back to these pleasant streets.

"I don't believe it!" she exclaimed when Peter had pulled in
and parked neatly in front of Gus's house. Street lamps and
varieties of Christmas lights glittered up and down the street,
illuminating the snow frosting each front yard.

"I know, my parking finesse dazzles most people."

"No, no, it's the house. I can't believe you grew up in the
Vermont farmhouse. That's what I've always called it. God,

I've always *loved* this house. There's even smoke coming out of the chimney. I just want you to know this porch is my fantasy of where I would like to have spent my childhood summers reading instead of sitting in a mildewed butterfly chair on the concrete slab behind our little ranch house in Cheshire."

"It's the oldest house on the street, I guess," Peter said, leaning across her to punch open the recalcitrant passenger door. "I don't think I read as much as you probably did as a child. When I think about summers here, I mostly remember dirt-bomb fights and stickball in the street and trespassing in Mrs. Minetti's backyard to get to the muddy creek that flows into the reservoir. It was pretty idyllic. I'm sorry we didn't somehow meet when we were kids."

"Oh, we probably did cross paths," Natalie said. "New Haven syndrome means we have only a degree or two of separation. I'm sure we know people in common, or go to the same dentist. How could you miss Whitney Dairy?"

"We do have a connection, though—I did know your work," Peter reminded her. "I might be one of your best customers. Hey, look sharp, eagle eye is already checking you out."

"You didn't tell me she was a looker, kiddo," boomed Gus, as he erupted out his front door onto the porch with such exuberance that Natalie was reminded of Drummer, her mother's slightly manic Airedale, acquired soon after her father's death. Lillian had loved him mightily. When Drummer was run over in his prime, a hit-and-run, Lillian was so heartbroken she said she would never have another dog.

Gus seized Natalie's hand and pumped it several times with his two hands and a damp dish towel, hauling her into his house. "You like artichokes, Natalie? There's an artichoke waiting for you with your name on it that's better than any artichoke you've ever tasted in your life."

"Wonderful! Thistles for dinner!" Natalie said. "*Cynara scolymus.*"

"Peter, don't you let her get away," ordered Gus. "I like this girl. Another autodidact like you and your old man. If you scare her off, I'll kill you. Come in, come in, both of you."

"Remind me, what's an autodidact?" Peter asked when they were settled in front of the fireplace with wine and a bowl of delicious oily black olives while Gus put the finishing touches on dinner.

"An autodidact is a person who knows what an autodidact is," Natalie replied. They both laughed. "Literally, a self-taught person. You must know that. Auto, self. Didact, informed person. The sort of person who knows about annealing silver and gold and can tell you the origins of voir dire and battalion."

"And why are you so specifically well-informed about artichokes?"

"I read up on thistles for some pieces I was working on a few years ago. I was a bit obsessed for a while. They're vegetables, until they flower and go to seed, when they're inedible. Or they're weeds, depending on who wants them. They have hearts. And a choke. And the leaves grow in a Fibonacci pattern. Anyway, my artichoke pieces ended up so abstract— big chased pins, mostly, and some earrings, with little diamonds and lapis lazuli inlays—that most people probably never noticed the thistle form. You probably wouldn't remember those."

Peter sat very still, looking down at the rug, his shoulders hunched. Natalie gazed across the room. Several family photos were ranged across the top of an upright piano. Curious, and to give him some space, she got up and walked over to take a closer look.

Of course there was the wedding picture, Peter and Sarah poised at the brink of a life they weren't going to have for very long. Peter looked a decade younger. Sarah was wearing a pair of Natalie's diamond and lapis lazuli thistle earrings. Knowing Sarah's fate, Natalie couldn't see around it, could only look at Sarah's picture and see a dead woman, someone whom time had already buried and rushed past.

"She loved those thistle earrings," Peter said. "She wore them all the time. I gave them to her for our wedding. Something blue."

"Dinner is ready whenever you are!" Gus sang out from the dining room just then.

By the end of dinner—the artichokes were, as promised, spectacularly delicious, garlicky and tender—Natalie had dismissed any of her fears that Gus was insufficiently civilized for Lillian, though she had begun to doubt that Lillian was lively enough for Gus. And Lillian could be, well, prickly. Thistly. Argumentative. Judgmental. Set in her ways. Who knows? It might work. He could be oblivious to her sandpaper personality, or just enjoy the challenge of charming a playful side out of her mother. How could Lillian not be swept off her feet, or at least, pleasantly tilted, by exuberant Gus? The Lewis men had charm. After all, look at Peter and Crazy Cello Lady, which had begun with outraged yelling.

"We lost Sarah a little over a year ago, you know," Gus confided to Natalie when Peter had gone into the kitchen for a second helping of Gus's superb rice pudding. "He's been really down this month, too, what with Christmas and all. I can't tell you what a difference you've made. He was just dreading it, this time last week. I was afraid it was going to get rough."

"Hey, no talking about absent parties," Peter scolded as he sat back down. "I'm right here. I can hear you."

"I was just inviting Natalie here to come over tomorrow night to keep the Lewis men company on Christmas Eve," Gus said. "And I think she agreed." Peter looked at Natalie questioningly.

"That sounds really nice, but I'm supposed to have dinner with my mother," Natalie said hesitantly.

"Great! Bring her along. The more the merrier."

This was too easy. They were supposed to be setting Gus up, not the other way around.

"I need to check with her—but it's just the two of us, nobody else, and I'm in charge of cooking dinner. So I'm pretty sure we can do it."

"That's set then. The neighborhood carolers get here around eight o'clock for my famous wassail bowl, so dinner will be later. I'm roasting a goose," Gus announced. "I always roast a goose. Basted with gin and orange juice, that's my secret. So you'll want to be here by seven-thirty for the caroling. Unless you want to come over earlier to help peel chestnuts. We zap them in the microwave—one of the few good reasons to have one of those infernal devices. Does your mother sing soprano or alto?"

"Dad, please, take a breath, give Natalie some space, for God's sake!"

"My mother is part Jewish, actually," Natalie said. "So I don't think she's done a lot of caroling—it's never been a tradition in our family. But I always loved the Christmas songs at school assemblies. And she likes to sing old show tunes, like Rodgers and Hart. She might enjoy it, in fact. I guess she's alto."

"It's settled then!" said Gus triumphantly. "You kids will work out any other details. No dressing up."

"But use discretion when selecting your attire," intoned Peter.

"I have to tell you, my mother's voice is better than mine—I sing in the cracks., pretty much," added Natalie. "I was the kid the music teacher assigns to the triangle, on the grounds that I don't have to make the sound, just attempt to guess at the beat. So between the two of us, I'm not sure what we would bring to the music part of your Christmas Eve tradition. If you don't think we should come tomorrow night, that's perfectly understandable. We could do it another time or something. Whatever."

"I'm not going to dignify that with an answer. Straighten her out while I make coffee, okay Peter?" Gus said cheerfully, heading for the kitchen. "It's all set then."

"I love trying to follow the way you get from one subject to the next," Peter said. "I'll have to see if I can locate a triangle for you, so you can keep the beat for all the carolers. You're lucky—I had to take clarinet lessons. From Mr. Fallon, who used to spit on my reed for me. Sarah didn't believe me, but he really did."

"I believe you. And talk about people whose trains of thought get rolling," Natalie laughed. "Gus is like Thomas the Tank Engine coming down the track! I don't see how you can complain about my associative mind. You know I think he's great, right? I really like Gus."

"And I really hope you will come tomorrow night," Peter said, "No one cares if you know the words. Or can carry a tune. Anyway, won't caroling on that porch fulfill some childhood fantasy of yours?" He smiled at her. "And we get Lillian and Gus together, which is the whole point of this enterprise, right? Say yes."

"You know, it's probably going to be a terrible match," Natalie cautioned over the sudden racket of Gus's coffee grinding. "I'm warning you, my mother is really impossible. This could be a truly terrible experiment that goes quite wrong." She leaned across the table to flick a crumb off Peter's sweater in a gesture that felt entirely right.

"Terrible," agreed Peter, catching her hand with one of his and holding it for a moment on the tablecloth. With his fingertip he traced the hammered surface of the twisted silver bangle on her wrist. "Out of the question. Idiotic. What can we be thinking? A lousy idea. Doomed to failure. I can't imagine why we ever thought it could possibly work."

Jane of Hearts

It is a joy to be hidden but a disaster not to be found.
—D.W. Winnicott

THEIR CRIMES WERE CRIMELESS. Or nearly so. Nobody was
home when they broke in and rambled around those houses
on Jane's street. They never caused any damage or left any
trace of their expeditions. An unlocked window or sliding
door, a key under the mat, or under a flowerpot on the back
steps—there was always a perfectly easy way for two children
to slip unnoticed inside the unoccupied houses in this neighborhood. Northbury, Connecticut, was both quiet and prosperous, and in the last, still days of the summer of 1982, the
only house on Jane's block of Spruce Street with a burglar
alarm belonged to the Dishers, an elderly childless couple on
the corner who never went further than the grocery store or a
doctor's appointment. (Neighbors would have been surprised
to know about their valuable inherited collection of gold dou-
bloons, some quite rare, thus the alarm.)

It was the middle of that parched August when Jane and
Tate started their secret missions. Though most of the year
Jane's street was full of children, the two of them were the only
ones around for the final desultory days of that school vacation
season, which stretched into September that year, when the
Labor Day weekend tide of returning families would bring
the neighborhood back to life. Even the usual dogs and cats

of Spruce Street were absent. The knobby-kneed mailman in his summer uniform shorts and pith helmet made his rounds every morning. So did some dog walkers from other nearby streets. Very early, on some of these mornings, Jane could hear through her open bedroom window the slap slap slap of the passing jogger, a man she didn't recognize, whose route included Spruce Street. It was so still that Jane could hear him when he stopped at the corner, jogging in place, to hawk and spit and take a swig from his water bottle before launching himself forward to resume his run. She liked knowing about him while he did not know about her.

In the afternoons there were fewer people to look out for. Jane and Tate made sure the coast was clear by cycling up and down the block in tandem, surveilling for delivery vans or door-to-door sellers. An Amway lady often parked on the shady side of Spruce Street at the end of the block, with the motor off and all her windows open. She just sat there in her brown sedan with its Amway bumper sticker ("Shop without going shopping!"). They tried to avoid riding past her and would change direction if they spotted her car in time to swerve away without being too obvious about it. The Amway lady always waved at Jane and Tate as if she knew them, though, of course, she didn't.

When she leaned out of her car window one day to beckon Jane, there was no avoiding her, so while Tate rode away, the ridiculous Ace of Spades he had clothes-pinned to the frame of his bicycle so it would flutter in the spokes whirring faster and faster, sounding like a dirt bike (he hoped), Jane coasted to a stop, her hand brakes squeaking. She circled around, bumping up onto the sidewalk on the driver's side, and even before she had come to a stop the Amway lady had asked Jane if her mother was home, was hers one of the houses on this pretty street, how lucky that she lived here, which house, and would her mother be interested in free samples of vitamins or did she know what cleaning products her mother liked to use?

Jane had no good answers, so she rode away without answering at all, standing on the pedals to go as fast as she could, feeling horribly ashamed of her own rudeness while also wishing she had a mother interested in free vitamins and cleaning supplies and a visit from the desperate Amway lady, or from anyone. After that, the Amway lady stopped parking on Spruce Street.

Jane's mother worked in the office of a Bridgeport insurance agency. She had taken the job after Jane's father moved out, when Jane was in fourth grade. Jane hadn't seen her father since then. Every now and then he sent her postcards with pictures of cactus and roadrunners on them, and once there was a jackalope, the scrawled message often beginning with Hiya Kiddo! or Dear Janie, which nobody had ever called her. So far there had been eleven postcards (though when she confronted him about this many years later, he would insist he had sent dozens). Jane tacked these up in an even row on the bulletin board over her desk, message side out, and when she observed to her mother that the handwriting was completely different from one to the next, Jane's mother looked at them and sighed and said that his tart of the month probably wrote the postcards for him.

Jane wondered if he knew (or would be interested in knowing, or would be interested in telling his tart of the month) that she was going into seventh grade, which meant she would be attending the Maple Avenue Middle School, riding the bus every morning instead of walking to the nearby elementary school as she had done since kindergarten. When she thought about the imminence of seventh grade, it was the daily bus rides that gave her disquietude. She hoped she wouldn't throw up. She hoped the new kids from the other two elementary schools in Northbury would be interesting and not unfriendly. Or failing that, not mean. At least Tina Bartlett, next door, was in her grade so she wouldn't be alone at the bus stop on the corner. Maybe they would walk to the bus stop together every morning, the way they had walked the five blocks together to Oak Elementary most mornings. Jane found her a little dull, irritating to play with, agreeable but unimaginative. She never said it, but they both knew that Tina Bartlett was her assistant. She missed her when the Bartletts went away as they did at the beginning and end of every summer.

The Bartlett sisters were a set of three graduated versions of one another. Melissa, who planned to be a famous actress (she starred in the high school play three years in a row), was the oldest. Then came Tina, the middle one. On their walks to and from Oak Elementary, Tina was responsible for her little sister. Anything Jane and Tina talked about, Heather would chime in, and then Tina would speed up impatiently, and Jane would match her stride, leaving Heather to lope behind them the rest of the way to school, catching up only at corners where they waited for her before they crossed the street.

(Northbury was one of many New England towns with streets named for varieties of indigenous trees, and while much of Spruce Street was punctuated by tall, dense Norway Spruce, owing to devastating blights there were no longer Elms on Elm Street or Chestnuts on Chestnut Avenue.)

When the three Bartlett girls were together, there was no mistaking which was which, but when Tina was apart from the others, at school or in the neighborhood, for the grown-ups who had never bothered to discern each of the sisters separately and simply knew them as those three Bartlett girls, she was inevitably the "now which one are you?" sister. There were lots of things Jane didn't like about being an only child, but each time someone asked Tina which Bartlett sister she was, Jane liked the sensation of her own singularity, like a struck middle C.

After school, in contrast to the chill and stillness of Jane's house, the Bartlett house always had the sweet aroma of Mrs. Bartlett's cookies or brownies, which she conjured up magi-

cally nearly every afternoon. Occasionally there was her apple-
sauce cake, which Jane liked, raisins and all, more than the
Bartlett sisters did. (Tina would always pluck out the raisins and leave them lined up around the rim of the plate.)
The cookies and brownies were always free for the taking,
it's an open invitation, Mrs. Bartlett had told Jane, who had
already discerned that much in the generous Bartlett household was free for the taking. The mitten basket hanging on
the wall beside the back door brimmed with a wild assortment of single mittens and gloves, tangled with mufflers that
once matched long-lost hats. Under the stairs there was a pile
of unpaired snow boots in an apple crate. Sometimes in winter Heather had clomped to school in two left boots. How
Jane in her matched mittens and boots scorned and envied the
Bartlett girls for this.

By late afternoon, when they were playing Twister down
in in their basement family room—where they also held
headstand competitions with old stuffed animal prizes, and
played a violent form of dodgeball with throw pillows, and
made messes of glitter and paint and glue in the sink next
to the washer and dryer—the savory tang of Bartlett family
dinner roasting in the oven or simmering on the stove made
Jane wish more than anything to be one of them, to blend
into their family as the fourth sister, the other middle sister nobody could tell from her sisters. She longed to take for
granted, as the three Bartlett girls did, every night's impending roast chicken, or pot roast or, on Wednesdays, spaghetti
(Mrs. Bartlett's predictability was thrilling to Jane), the sauce
bubbling in a saucepan on the back burner while the big pot
of boiling spaghetti water steamed up the kitchen windows.

Just as the cooking aromas reached a crescendo of desirabil-
ity that Jane inhaled deeply but could hardly bear (though the
Bartlett girls seemed oblivious and unmoved), Mrs. Bartlett
would stand at the top of the basement stairs to call down
that dinner was in ten minutes and it was somebody's turn to

set the table. Each time they all racketed up the stairs toward the kitchen, Jane willed Mrs. Bartlett to see how much she wanted to stay for dinner. If only she would invite Jane to pull up another chair at their big kitchen table with its red checked oilcloth that squeaked in a particular way when wiped clean. As she ladled and scooped food into serving bowls while her daughters set the table, Mrs. Bartlett would remind the girls that they had to get their homework done right after dinner, taking turns at the piano for a half hour practice time each, or there would be no TV, and then the front door would open at the same time every night, just as dinner was going on the table, and that would mean it was six o'clock and Mr. Bartlett was home.

Jane was embarrassed, the times she lingered too long, when Mr. Bartlett was already in the front hall taking off his necktie before she had slipped out the back door by the kitchen, those occasions when Mrs. Bartlett had to remind her that she should go home now, her mother was probably waiting to serve dinner too. Mrs. Bartlett had apparently never noticed that Jane's mother was very rarely home by six. (The kindest people weren't necessarily perfect noticers, Jane had concluded, because they assumed that other people were as thoughtful as they were.) Jane knew very well that whenever her mother did come home, there would not be anything resembling a Bartlett family dinner on their pocked kitchen table that was heaped at one end with library books and piles of mail, but she kept that a secret and always pretended to agree with Mrs. Bartlett. Jane's mother didn't like her job at the insurance agency, but it paid the rent (few people in this neighborhood of homeowners knew they rented their house), and it was the best she could do with her limited qualifications, she had explained to Jane, until she finished her night course at the community college. Then she could try to get a better job as a paralegal at a law office somewhere, maybe in New Haven, a nicer commute.

Jane did not want any of the Bartletts to find out that she and her mother subsisted on microwaved frozen dinners, and not always at the same time, though sometimes there was Chinese takeout in white cardboard boxes with thin wire handles and they would sit together, lingering over the food. Every now and then, on the best nights, Jane's mother got home a little early, with a warm rotisserie chicken leaking through its insulated foil bag onto the counter. This was Jane's favorite. Because she had thought it was called "roast history" chicken when she was little, this was what she and her mother still called it. Jane loved the cozy feeling of their roast history chicken nights, which reminded her (and maybe reminded her mother, too) of the family dinners they used to have.

That summer Jane felt herself untethered, floating with nowhere to go. Was this being at loose ends? What did that mean, really? Her house was oppressively full of nothing. With her mother either at the insurance agency or preoccupied with studying to become a paralegal so she could earn more money, studying the vacant house next door became a preoccupation for Jane. She would populate the Bartlett house in her mind, in a sequence of scenes, like a scripted dream. She would begin at the ancient upright piano in the front room with Tina, or perhaps one of the other sisters, by playing four-hand "Heart and Soul" or "Chopsticks" (ever since the music teacher at school told the class that the composer intended for the piece to be played with the bottom pinky-finger edges of the hands, in a chopping motion, Jane played it precisely that way).

Then, where was Mrs. Bartlett? At the stove in the kitchen, now summoning the three girls to wash up and set the table for dinner, and here comes Mr. Bartlett, walking in the front door with his briefcase, setting it down, taking off his necktie. Where would Jane, the omniscient narrator, insert herself in this familial tableau? Did she have to leave already on that

cue, was she being exiled from her own story? No. Helping to
set the table? At the stove beside Mrs. Bartlett, tasting something delicious at the end of a wooden spoon in order to agree
that it was just right? She was only delaying the inevitable.
She wouldn't be invited to sit down with them and have dinner. This was always the moment when she would be gently
invited to go home. Her imagination failed her when she tried
to write herself more deeply into the Bartlett family story.

It was an interminable and lonely final stretch of summer.
The weather was unusually hot and humid. There had been
no rain in weeks. All the leaves on the trees were wilting and
fading early. Lawns had turned to straw. The fresh sparkle of
summer and all its promises when school let out had evaporated and was now replaced by relentless, baking heat, skies
darkening earlier every night, and back to school this and
back to school that. How can you go back to a school you
have never attended? Jane liked to find the incongruencies
and inconsistencies in slogans and phrases. When her mother
asked her if she wanted more of the Chinese bean curd (why
was her mother always, always, always surprised that Jane just
didn't like bean curd? The texture reminded her of inedible
things like paste and soap and modeling dough) Jane would
invariably reply I haven't had any so how can I take more?
If her mother wasn't distracted, she would give the correct
answer: You can always take more than nothing. It was one of
Jane's favorite Alice scenes, and it was a useful way to lure her
mother into being present.

With all the other families on the street away, Jane had
noticed that there was just one other kid around, a boy with
an eye patch who must live nearby. Jane had never seen him
before he started coasting past her house over and over, slow-
ing down on the approach and then speeding up. He was
riding a blue girls' bicycle that made a fluttering sound as it
passed because of a card attached to the frame that brushed

the turning spokes of the rear tire. He was circling the block, appearing and reappearing. Then he vanished. Jane longed to discuss him with Tina, who would have agreed (the way she agreed with everything Jane proposed) that he was new, and odd, and was the card in the spokes admirable or ludicrous (Jane did like the riffling sound it made), and surely he was someone to keep under surveillance, someone to follow if he reappeared. She planned to start a notebook on blue bicycle eye patch boy.

Jane was filled with something, but she didn't know what it was. Did other people fill up with this big balloon of pressured nothing feeling, and did they understand it? She wasn't entirely certain that other people were as alive as she was. Where was the evidence? Did she have to remain suspended in wait for the return of the Bartlett family in order to . . . well, what, exactly? In order to do the opposite of expand, in order to feel just the right amount of gravity. How long would she have to wait? Tina had told her they kept a back door key hidden in case of emergencies, under the heavy concrete pot of dirt at the bottom of the back steps that had previously held dying geraniums, and before that, geraniums. The emergency of missing the Bartletts was Jane's invitation. The key was exactly where Tina had said it would be, in a plastic sandwich bag, there for the taking.

The first time she went into the uninhabited Bartlett house on her own, Jane closed the back door soundlessly and then walked around carefully, visiting each room, gliding her fingers over the piano keys lightly, stopping when a couple of notes sounded faintly. There were only ant traps on the kitchen counters. The house was eerily quiet without the crosscurrents of Bartlett family presence; nevertheless it was rich with the nextdoorness she craved. Jane lay down in the middle of the living room, on the thick carpet that always had pleasing vacuum cleaner patterns across its surface like shoreline ripples in the sand when the tide has receded. She starfished her arms and legs a few times to make a carpet angel. When she turned her head she could see a single forgotten pink sneaker lying on its side under the sofa.

Upstairs, Jane lay down again, this time on Tina's bed. The room was abnormally neat, with everything put away. There was a large white scallop shell full of Tina's various hair clips and barrettes and elastics on the table next to her bed, a scrubbed exception to the seashell rule. Mrs. Bartlett's family shared a small, damp, tarpaper cabin just two blocks from the public beach in Westerly, Rhode Island, which they had the use of every summer, in the first week of July. They returned with peeling sunburns and buckets of big, sandy broken nautilus and whelk shells that Mrs. Bartlett had permitted in the car but then made them leave outside and away from the house because the rotting seaweed trapped inside the chambered hearts of those beautiful shells emitted a foul odor that she deemed quite unbeautiful. Mrs Bartlett also banned any treasured husks of horseshoe crabs from crossing her threshold, so these, too, were lined up under the hedge that delineated their backyard. (Roaming dogs took occasional interest in the pungent emanations of these carcasses and would carry off the odd horseshoe crab. Somewhere, a perplexed homeowner would find the chewed remains in a yard.)

Jane got up and went over to the big glass jar on Tina's dresser that was filled with sea glass shards, mostly various shades of green, punctuated with blue and brown specimens, and just a few red crumbs of smooth glass at the bottom, all collected diligently by Tina over several summers. She had a rule for her collection, keeping only the pieces that were fully frosted all over, throwing back into the surf the bits of glass that were not yet fully transformed and worn down by the roll and tumble of the sea. Tina's sea glass collection was her prize possession. Sometimes she and Jane would dump out the jar onto her quilt and arrange the pieces by color, size, and shape.

Jane thought the best piece was a green shard that was nearly heart-shaped, though Tina's favorite was a pale aquamarine ring, big enough for her thumb, that had been transformed by the ocean from the top lip of a bottle.

Jane could see her own bedroom window from here. Tina had probably never bothered to observe Jane. She was not as interested in Jane as Jane was interested in the Bartletts, individually and collectively. She wandered the hallway, opening the door to the linen closet to see all the sheets and towels folded neatly in stacks. The door was then difficult to close, and she had to push it several times until it clicked and held. She did not want to leave a telltale open door. Though Jane had not loved her three years in the Girl Scouts, numerous little phrases or songs she had been required to recite floated through her mind at odd moments. *Take nothing but pictures, leave nothing but footprints, kill nothing but time.* But not even footprints. She returned to the living room, where she effaced her carpet angel by shuffling across it in small steps until it was no longer distinct.

In Mr. and Mrs. Bartlett's bedroom, there was a huge closet filled with thick layers of heavy dark clothing, which swayed and brushed Jane as she crawled all the way to the back of the closet, where Mr. Bartlett's shoes were stacked like firewood. Tina told Jane that her father said he just could never part with old shoes and so here they all were, every pair he had ever owned.

Every Bartlett fact and artifact fascinated Jane. This closet with its cedar plank walls was as familiar to her as any other room in this house. It was always the optimal (though obvious) hiding place for games of sardines, sometimes big games, involving other kids from the neighborhood, since it was so capacious. If only they could push through the back to tumble out into snowy Narnia. How they had tried. Once Jane told Heather that she and Tina had actually succeeded and were in fact just back from a long Narnia adventure, one of many they had secretly accomplished, which had made Heather sob and then wail in despair so loudly at having been left behind that Mrs. Bartlett came sprinting up the stairs, worried that some-one had slammed a hand in a door or worse. Jane and Tina finally convinced Heather, while she sat hiccupping on her mother's lap, that it wasn't really true, and they had gone no further than the back of the closet. Mr. Bartlett's scary shoe collection made her want to scream about that closet too, Mrs. Bartlett said, soothing her youngest child.

She crawled out of the stuffy closet onto the rug in front of the mirrored bathroom door and lay there, cooling off. How long had she been in there? The room was dim, with shad-ows falling across the rug, the light coming through the vene-tian blinds forming a crenellated pattern. Jane loved to draw castles with crenellated turrets. It was a word she liked. She had killed nothing but time, indeed. When she got up to go, before she went back downstairs to slip out the back door and replace the key exactly where she had found it, some impulse made Jane scoop the contents of the lumpy glazed bowl (made by one of her daughters for Mother's Day) that sat on Mrs. Bartlett's bedside table. Into the pocket of her shorts, where the smooth, heart-shaped green shard of sea glass from Tina's jar was already nestled, went a collar button from one of Mr. Bartlett's office shirts, a thimble, a square green Monopoly house, a red and white marble, a bobby pin, a blue glass bead, a Canadian penny. When she was outside, the slanting light of late afternoon was somehow unexpected, the way it is when you leave a movie theater and walk out into daylight.

It was reasonable for Jane to go inside the Bartletts' house while they were away, keeping an eye on things. It was an act of devotion. It felt necessary, the way watering a plant is nec-essary. She needed to do this. Jane returned the next day. And the next. It became her daily ritual, a secret mission to accomplish each day, a way of counting off the days before summer's end, when school would begin and the Bartletts would be back home where they belonged.

The boy with the eye patch riding the blue girl's bicycle was back. After his third revolution around the block, Jane waited for him, standing astride her own bike. She could hear the zipping card sound before he rounded the corner. When he appeared, she let him pass and then pedaled after him. They rode around the block together, without speaking, with him in the lead, and then they went around again, and again. The third time around, he stopped in front of a house on the street that was behind Jane's and dismounted, flinging the bicycle onto the grass. It had no kickstand. He went to the side of the house and turned on the water spigot. He picked up the end of the hose from which water began to stream and took a long slurping drink.

Hose water, he offered. Sure. Jane took some big gulps of the hose water, which was nearly hot from sitting in the long coil of hose that had been baking in the sun. Somehow, once she decided it was just weird garden hose tea, she didn't really mind it. They stood together in comfortable silence. The water gushing from the hose began to run cold, and they took turns drinking it again.

He told her he was visiting his grandmother for the rest of the summer. Jane looked at the front of his house and realized that she knew his grandmother—Jane and the Bartlett girls circled their own block first thing every Halloween before branching out to adjacent blocks. When Heather had been really little, that circuit around the block was the limit of her trick or treating. Once they had delivered her back home, where they rang the doorbell as if it were any other house, the older girls were delighted to be less impeded by her dawdling and complaining as they made their efficient rounds of the best streets in the neighborhood, the ones with elaborate

Halloween decorations and adults who answered the door in
costumes and gave full-size candy bars. The nice lady from
the bakery who gave out big plastic-wrapped black and white
cookies lived here—she was Tate's grandmother. The cookies
were good—they were from Lorraine's, where she worked—
but nevertheless disappointing, like apples or boxes of raisins,
on Halloween.

Northbury had a small commercial center adjacent to the
town green, with just a few shops, flanked by two banks.
There were two churches on the town green, and a town hall,
and a library. These four stately buildings anchoring the center of each side of the square town green reminded Jane of
the four Railroad lines on a Monopoly board: Short, B&O,
Pennsylvania, Reading. But there were an increasing number
of empty storefronts, a sad inevitability given the nearby mall.
The coffee shop only served breakfast and lunch. The phar-
macy that had been on the corner for fifty years would probably close when the proprietor retired, now that most people
preferred the huge, brightly lit chain drugstores that were
open late, cheaper, and also sold beach balls and groceries.

There was one clothing store, a dreary little dress shop run
by a severe-looking woman who sat behind the counter reading a book, though she would look up and stare whenever Jane
looked in the window, which made Jane so uncomfortable she
had never gone through the door, even when she was looking for a small Mother's Day gift that she might have found
there, like a hair clip or headband. But everything in the window always looked as if it was meant for schoolteachers. The
shop seemed stuck in the past. Even—especially—the name,
Whistle Bait.

The cold white hands of the mannequin in the window
of Whistle Bait were reversed. Once she had noticed this,
just before Christmas, every time Jane passed by the little dress shop where her mother had once bought a jacket

on sale (marked down most likely because of its unflattering pale orange creamsicle color), Jane automatically checked to see if this had been corrected. All winter the mannequin had been dressed in a long tweed coat with big buttons, a jaunty beret cocked over her blank face. Below her bent right arm, a wrong hand was artfully tucked halfway into a side pocket, giving the coat a stylish drape. In spring, the mannequin wore a sleeveless yellow dress dotted with tiny, sprigged flowers, her white plastic shoulder hinges not completely covered by the fabric. The same bent right arm was now raised to hold the top of a broad-brimmed straw hat with that wrong hand, as if a breeze might otherwise blow it askew.

When Jane and her mother went into Lorraine's Butter-cake Bakery, which was across the street from the dress shop, Jane was always allowed to pick something, anything. But nothing she chose ever tasted as good as the bakery smelled. What was it, which bakery item in the trays that filled the glass cases gave the bakery that intoxicating buttery aroma? The poppy seed kolachi? Their signature buttercake with the cinnamon streusel topping? The babka? The apple macaroon cake? The gooey schnecken? The raisin walnut coffee cake? The apple strudel? The rich, flakey mille-feuille nobody could pronounce so they were now called custard slices? Surely not the birthday cakes. Whatever it was, Jane wanted that one. The very word "buttercake" was a promise. Kitty, the woman behind the counter that afternoon (Jane now matched this familiar face—she was Tate's grandmother) had laughed and told her that many people had made this request, but the truth was that even if you got one of every single thing in the case, every item that was baked at Lorraine's, you would never cap-ture the buttery fragrance.

Jane loved to watch how the white box with the famil-iar Lorraine's logo in diagonal red script across the top was wrapped with practiced hands by Tate's grandmother, or one of the high school girls who worked there on weekends, or by

Mr. and Mrs. Fischer, the couple who owned and lived over the bakery in an apartment that was surely redolent of the elusive buttery fragrance. They often spoke to each other in a German dialect that was their first common language where they had met, in Alsace-Lorraine, thus the name of the bakery. People in Northbury assumed they were German (though she was Russian, and he was Hungarian) and some people called her Lorraine (her name was Olga). Both descended from families of bakers, and some of Stefan Fischer's pastries were attempts to re-create the ethereal strudels and flakey cinnamon twists for which his family's bakery and café had been known in Budapest before the war.

Though Olga's father, Sergei, had been a soldier in the Russian army in his youth, his too was a baker's heritage, and when he was wounded during a skirmish in the summer of 1918 (about which he was circumspect for the rest of his life, confiding only in his wife Katerina, Olga's mother), he returned from the army to the family bread-baking trade. By the time Olga was born, he was renowned in Kuznetsovsk for his rye and pumpernickel loaves.

Red and white twisted baker's twine issued from an ancient cast-iron dispenser hanging high over the counter. Wrap wrap loop loop tie pull into bows cut. *Hier ist dein Gebäck.* Here are your pastries. *Itt vannak a süteményeid.* Jane could watch and watch some more, box after box, the lightning-quick wrap wrap loop loop, but she still didn't quite see how they did it. It was like watching a card trick.

The boy with the eye patch submitted to Jane's interview. Name? Tate Baldwin. Age? Eleven. Why the eye patch? He was supposed to wear it all day, every day. He had promised his parents he would do it while he was staying with his grandmother. This was the last chance to try to fix his lazy eye, by covering his other hardworking eye, to force the lazy eye to wake up and see better. This deprived him of depth perception. For this reason, Tate was permitted to circle his own block on bicycle, but he could go no further. His grandmother wished he wouldn't ride his mother's old bicycle at all, but she couldn't really forbid it, with so few other options for Tate that summer. She worried that he could misjudge the distance between his own soft and breakable eleven-year-old body and the hard, unyielding and fast-moving fenders of approaching cars as he crossed an intersection. Of course, there was no way to protect a child from every possible misjudgment, but if he just circled his own block, surely that would be safest. So around the block he went, clockwise, over and over. Then he would reverse and go counterclockwise, for the same number of revolutions. Winding and unwinding the invisible string that trailed behind him wherever he went, every day of his life. He tried to keep it even. He tried to keep count. He had tried to make his mother's old bicycle more like a boy's bicycle with the Ace of Spades fluttering in the spokes of the rear wheel.

They sat in the shade on Jane's front steps drinking from plastic tumblers of iced tea from the pitcher in Jane's refrigerator. Her mother mixed it with orange juice, which sounded repulsive but tasted good. Tate's family lived in Chicago, he said, right by the lake that was as big as an ocean, (Jane didn't disagree, though she had done a report on the Great Lakes in fifth grade), but right now he was staying with his grandmother for the rest of the summer because.

Because? He hesitated. Because of the secret. He wasn't supposed to tell anyone. Jane waited.

Okay. But you really, really can't tell anyone. His father was an accountant. A Certified Public Accountant. Tate revealed this proudly, the way someone might mention that his father was an astronaut. (He didn't really know what this meant. Jane didn't either.) His father the Certified Public Accountant was testifying in a criminal trial, he whispered without turning his head, as if they were under surveillance and were trying to act natural. Tate had heard more than he was meant to hear as a stealthy eavesdropper on the stairs after he was supposed to be asleep. He knew his father was scared because he had done accountant work for someone in the garbage business who turned out to be a criminal and there was something about garbage trucks and illegal dumping and corrupt permits and toxic waste and union officials and city contracts and a bad judge (whatever that was) and there were some people who were supposed to testify in court like Tate's father but instead they had disappeared.

It was the disappearing that led to Tate's parents making this sudden plan. They explained with false cheer that they had decided to take him to stay with his grandmother in Connecticut where he would be safely out of harm's way, just for now. It would be for a little while, and then when his father's part of the trial was over they were going to move, to go live somewhere else, where he would have a new school and make new friends. It was going to be a surprise not just for Tate but for his parents, too.

Tate kept thinking about the phrase his mother had used when she explained the abrupt long drive to Connecticut with all his clothes, starting in the middle of the night, for this unexpected visit with Granny Kit—where he would be "out of harm's way." Tate wasn't sure what being *in* harm's way would mean, but he liked his grandmother, who brought nice things home from the bakery every day in a white box tied with red and white string, and he liked sleeping in his mother's childhood bedroom with its bookcase full of books in which she had written her name, Barbara Welch, her juvenile handwriting showing signs of turning into the way she still wrote her name now.

He was happy to pass uncounted hours rambling around his grandmother's house, looking at things in every room where his mother grew up, his imaginary lifelong string unspooling behind him, crisscrossing the rooms like a cat's cradle as he wandered all three floors of the house. He would have to miss the last few vision therapy appointments that had been scheduled back in Chicago, but he could use the rest of the summer at Granny Kit's to wear his eye patch all day. If he had to wear the patch, he didn't mind going to Connecticut where nobody knew him and nobody would make fun of him or speak in pirate talk or say Ahoy, Matey!

His parents had worked out the rules for his solitary afternoons when his grandmother was at the bakery, a job she loved because it got her out of the house. He was a mature enough eleven-year-old to spend a few hours unsupervised, the family had agreed. When he was home alone, Tate was not allowed to turn on the stove or answer the door. He was allowed to play in the yard, a square of weed-punctuated grass hemmed by overgrown barberry bushes with very sharp thorns. After one afternoon of tossing a petrified pink rubber ball (which he had found in the basement) into the sky and catching it a few million times, he was done with that. He had made himself dizzy, which had made him miss catching the ball, which rolled out of sight, and then he was stabbed by the barberry thorns while retrieving it. How and what exactly did his sweet grandmother imagine he would "play" out there on his own?

Tate was allowed to watch television, though he rarely turned it on. Daytime television was boring, and Granny Kit didn't have very many channels, and no matter how the rabbit ears antennae on top of the set were aimed, the picture was always grainy (which was like seeing with his weak eye). Ordinarily, Tate liked to read and was a fast reader, but the eye patch made that challenging, because his lazy eye made the words on the page just as dim and fuzzy as the boring TV shows, and it took too long to read a page this way. He was tempted to take off the patch and read, but then his lazy eye would never work harder.

There was a limp old deck of cards in a drawer of the coffee table, and he liked to lay these out in patterns, arranging them in various orders. When Granny Kit asked him if he was playing solitaire he had agreed that he was, though he didn't know how to play it, but it sounded a lot like solitary, and he was definitely making up solitary arranging games with the cards, sometimes laying them out to follow the patterns in the carpet. (The Ace of Spades was missing, as it was clipped to his mother's old bicycle, and if he added a second card, for an even louder motorcycle effect, he had already chosen the Jack of Hearts, even though it would disrupt the symmetry of the four royal families.)

Alone on those afternoons (this he did not tell Jane), when he had satiated his card-arranging desires, he often played with the wooden train set. He understood he should have outgrown it, but he still loved the clack of connection between the simple smooth birch train cars, which were joined by magnets. He was glad to find it, to rediscover an old friend from when he was much younger. He couldn't remember why it was here in the closet in Granny Kit's house. Maybe it had migrated here from Chicago during some visit when it had been brought along so he would have something to occupy himself. The only child tax, his father had called it.

Jane had also been expected from an early age to occupy herself on numerous occasions. Who else would I occupy but myself? she had challenged her mother. Who else could I possibly occupy? Whom else, her mother non-answered. Don't get carried away. Who would carry me away? You tend to carry yourself away, said her mother.

Fitting the wooden train tracks together to form a pleasing series of loops and intersections in Granny Kit's living room, Tate recalled the familiar sensation of lying on this thick patterned carpet when he was younger, while the rest of the family were still eating dinner (was it Christmas? Thanksgiving?), trying to gaze at the trains from eye level, smallifying himself down to the same scale, as if he could be a tiny engineer inside the solid block of wood that was the locomotive pulling one of these trains. Now he added a long detour around the coffee table, glad to have so many straights and curves to work with so that he could make the complex layout flow without resorting to dead ends or off ramps into a carpet abyss. The train car magnet connectors were endlessly pleasing. If any one of the plain smooth freight cars was reversed, there was an invisible force field between the mismatched magnets that could drive the next car forward in front of the train with a magical gap, the cars never touching.

Tate had soldiered along in this solitary routine of bicycling around the block and playing with the wooden trains he was too old for and wandering in the house for a week before he and Jane spoke the first time. After a couple of days of riding their bicycles in loops around the block, they branched out to starting back-to-back and riding off in opposite directions in order to pass each other at the halfway point on the far side of the block, and then meet again where they had started, usually in front of Jane's house. It was a diverting variation for a day or two, and then it was as boring as everything else. They found an alley that ran behind four of the houses and they circled those houses that way for a while, but the unpaved alley was potholed and not worth the detour.

What else can we do? Is there anywhere else we can go, Tate asked. On this block, I mean.

Maybe. Jane regarded him solemnly. She hesitated. Could he be trusted? He was only eleven. But who would he tell?

I told you my secret.

Okay. I have a secret, too. It's big. Are you ready for a secret mission?

Jane and Tate might as well have been invisible as they slipped inside one house after the other, usually no more than two on the same day. These homes were all unoccupied while the families who lived in them were at their beach houses (the Pasterns and the Trenchards, who went to Old Black Point, where they also lived next door to each other), or up in Vermont (the van Dycks, whose departure was always heralded by a pair of sideways canoes strapped to the roof of their Volvo station wagon), or at the Jersey shore (the Sperrys, whose children claimed to get free Sperry Topsiders, which was a lie, though their grandfather Armstrong was indeed the brother of the boat shoe inventor), or on the Cape (the Gradys, the Cravens, the Snows), or on Nantucket (the Flannagans, whose startling row of backyard garden gnomes made Jane and Tate feel watched). Three families on the block were in two places at once, which is to say the children were at sleepaway camps in New Hampshire and Vermont while the parents were on a barge cruise in France (the Jaspers), on a Napa Valley wine-tasting tour (the Corrigans), or at a child-free resort in Puerto Vallarta (the Baileys).

Because the Bartletts were visiting those cousins in the Berkshires, the station car Mr. Bartlett drove each day and parked at the train station was parked at the top of the driveway in front of their old garage that was full of junk. Whenever he was home, the station car was parked in the driveway behind their long Country Squire station wagon, so anyone walking by had to step off the sidewalk into the street to get around it. But now the Country Squire had been packed up and driven away to the cousins in Otis, Massachusetts, who lived near an egg farm that Tina had complained to Jane about because the chicken shit smell on certain days was disgusting. The customarily blocked sidewalk in front of the Bartletts' house was unimpeded.

Jane and Tate only took little things on these excursions. These objects had no particular value, though once taken, the poker chips, seashells, dominoes, buttons, marbles, hotel sewing kits, dice, foreign coins, shards of sea glass, thimbles, binder clips, Monopoly houses, lipsticks, magnets, playing cards, rhinestones, postage stamps, cribbage pegs, river pebbles, collar stays, arcade tokens, chess pieces, hairpins, beads, pen nibs, and golf pencils that people abandon in bowls and drawers and ashtrays around their houses became the precious charms and talismans of their growing hoard. It was their valuable secret collection, their priceless filched treasure.

The first time Jane led Tate inside the Bartletts' house, he was appropriately in awe of her finesse with the hidden key, the checking to make sure the coast was clear, her slow, silent closing of the back door until it clicked quietly. Leading Tate from room to room, Jane felt like a tour guide in a museum. In a way, she was exactly that. She described everything she could think to describe about the Bartlett family, what they were each like, how they lived their lives in these hallowed rooms. She let Tate choose the talisman of the day, and he selected a smooth red poker chip from the flat dish on Mr. Bartlett's chest of drawers that also held collar stays, paper-wrapped toothpicks, a Kennedy half dollar, and several books of matches. They discussed the difference between stealing and borrowing. They were borrowers. She taught him the meaning of the word talisman.

Tate crawled behind her into the deep bedroom closet obediently, and sat cross-legged beside her under the swaying, plastic-shrouded winter clothes. When she breathed in the closet air, sweet with cedar and a faint sillage of Mrs. Bartlett's perfume, he too inhaled deeply. They sat together in the closet companionably, eyes closed. He was the *best* assistant. Together, they were capable of anything.

Tate followed Jane, slipping out the back door after her and keeping watch as she replaced the key exactly where it came from. When they were out on the sidewalk in front of Jane's house, where their bikes lay on the crisp tufts of parched lawn, Tate's eyes were sparkling. He wondered which house they would go to next time.

Oh. Let's make a map and a list, said Jane.

Each day they met in Jane's garage in front of their hoard, to make a plan. Jane had taken a little spiral notebook with a plaid cover from Tina's older sister Melissa's room. It made the perfect logbook for their missions. First they discussed and decided on their target house. Next, they bicycled slowly up and down the street, la la la, just two kids out biking on a hot summer afternoon, doing a reconnoiter to make sure they were unobserved. Then came the shivery butterflies moment of finding the way in (the ingress, Tate called it, the opposite of the way out, the egress, even if it was the same door). The most dangerous moment was this one—locating the key or open window, and then eeling and sliding and slipping inside the mission target. This rarely took more than five minutes, between the emergency keys that were easily located in the most obvious hiding places, high or low, and the unlocked windows and sliding doors.

Only once did they fail to find a way into a house, the van Dycks having been exceptionally thorough in their locking up. They had either hidden their emergency key too well or there wasn't one. But their garage, sitting at the end of their gravel driveway beyond the house, had yielded a wealth of brass washers, a baby food jar filled with bright copper flashing nails, a bucket of golf tees, a cloudy plastic box with fishing flies in every compartment, and some pleasingly heavy lug nuts from the wheels of a car. There was a rusted set of shelves filled with mahogany and cedar cigar boxes with Spanish lettering on the tops and fronts (Dr. van Dyck's father had been a cigar aficionado and a pack rat). Many of these contained exactly what the wood-burned block letters on the front edge promised: SCREWS, NAILS, HOOKS, HINGES. The prize of the day lay inside a large mahogany cigar box labelled on its front edge WOOD BURNING TOOL. Inside was a woodburning pen, accompanied by a tattered sheet of instructions. Jane and Tate made a list in the plaid notebook of all the garages they had overlooked before now, for future missions.

They did not break windows or jimmy locks. That was their policy. Jane and Tate only visited the houses that were so easily breached they had practically been invited in. Twice they found side or kitchen doors that had simply been left unlocked. There were two screened porches with unlocked doors leading to the next unlocked door to the house. Some people never bothered to lock their doors unless they went out of town, let alone their garages. Tate didn't lock Granny Kit's house when he biked around the block or when they were on these missions. He didn't even have a key. It was a very trusting, low-crime neighborhood.

They set a fifteen-minute limit, moving through the rooms together, having agreed that they would not split up after an unfortunate incident on the third day of their missions when they had been roaming silently through the Cravens' house, one upstairs and one downstairs, when they each heard the other's movements—a creaking floorboard, the squeak of a closet door—and so both believed that some member of the Craven family had come home unexpectedly. Though they had no coordinated plan for this (a tactical oversight that Jane regretted), Jane and Tate had instantly gone to ground. Tate slid under a bed. Jane stood motionless behind the heavy floor-length velvet curtains in the living room. They were only ghosts. The house was quiet for what felt like an eternity (it was twenty minutes) before Jane cautiously stepped out from the sweltering, airless alcove, her hair sticking to her face, which streamed with sweat. Do ghosts get bored when there is nobody to haunt? She gave a low whistle, and a moment later heard a matching whistled reply.

That afternoon, having retreated to the back corner of Jane's garage with the Craven treasures they had each chosen (a mahjong tile and a key), they proposed and ratified an official signal—their two-note whistle, like a cardinal. Like a doorbell. E and C, Tate had said matter-of-factly, surprising Jane, who wrote it down. That was when they also proposed and ratified by unanimous vote the three essential new rules for missions, which Jane also wrote down carefully. No more than fifteen minutes per domicile. Stay together. If caught, lie. Sometimes you have to lie.

At first they kept their hoard in a cigar box from the van Dycks' garage, and then in two cigar boxes from the van Dycks' garage, both with hinged lids, and then, in a week's time, when the collection was further augmented, they sorted the newest acquisitions into a flat wooden Coca-Cola crate, the kind with twenty-four compartments. (This they had rescued from the Trenchards' basement.) When they had a dozen cigar boxes and the Coca-Cola crate filled with completed mission inventory, Jane and Tate spent hours on their knees in the cool dim corner of Jane's garage where, at the end of each afternoon, they stacked them up beside a heap of rotting sacks that leaked moldy grass seed and sour fertilizer. (These, along with a bucket of rusted trowels and cultivators, a red gasoline can, and a cracked plastic snow shovel, had been there since Jane was a toddler, when they had moved into this house with Jane's father, pre tart of the month.)

After a mission accomplished, they would convene in the garage, lay out the cigar boxes, open the lids (some were hinged, some had separate sliding tops), and commence organizing and reorganizing their loot, their borrowings, making rules and adding meaning and wrangling over layouts and taking inventory at the end of each day. Sometimes they divided their artifacts into separate collections. The very best of these went into the two best cigar boxes, the ones with dovetailed corners and red velvet liner sheets and Punch Double Corona (Jane's) and Cohiba (Tate's) on the lids. Tate spent several afternoons printing, letter by letter, their names on these, using the woodburning tool, which smoked and gave off a pungent burning odor.

It was peaceful and still in the garage, and though sometimes they bickered over the rules of Blink, the elaborate game they were in the process of inventing (the Blink rules were in the plaid notebook that was their mission log, as well as their hoard inventory), entire afternoons passed while they hardly spoke at all as they sifted and sorted their collection. Blink was played across several cigar boxes and multiple checkerboards. So far, it required a variety of game tokens, dice, four different decks of cards, poker chips, backgammon pieces, a cribbage board with its pegs, and a complex arrangement of marbles, keys, coins, buttons, and Scrabble tiles across a Parcheesi board, a backgammon board, and four checkerboards. They had not yet actually played Blink. Their devotion was to the development of procedures, rules, protocols. The silent spell they cast over themselves for hours would be broken finally, just when the sun had gotten lower, casting the garage in shadow, by the *chup-chup-chup-chup-sssss-chup-chup-chup-chup-sssss* of the Flannagans' automated lawn sprinklers that popped up and went on at dusk each day.

There was a town-wide ban on watering lawns that summer of drought, and even the washing of cars with a running hose was not permitted, but still the Flannagans maintained their emerald lawns, which were mowed every so often by a uniformed crew of landscapers with huge, noisy mowers. There was a hand-painted sign nailed to a tree in front of the Flannagans' house, LAWN WATERED FROM OUR WELL, which went up just before they left for Nantucket. Theirs was the only green lawn in the neighborhood. Jane's mother questioned the existence of this well. Most of Northbury had converted to city water and sewers some twenty years ago. Was this lawn-water well extant, from the time when each house had its own well and septic system? There had been no new well-drilling. Her mother's suspicion fascinated Jane. She made a note. This was something to investigate with Tate. (She had no idea what they would look for and how they could determine the truth of the matter.) Wouldn't that be something, discovering a Flannagan crime? She had not liked Teddy Flannagan, who was a grade ahead of her, since the Halloween he and his older brother had thrown eggs at Jane's house. The stains etched in the paint were still visible in certain light.

If Tate hopped on his bicycle the moment the Flannagans' sprinklers sprang to life at the end of each afternoon, he could coast home just ahead of Granny Kit, who liked the exercise of her ten-minute walk home from Lorraine's Buttercake Bakery. Tate's grandmother tried to find a moment during her shifts to phone him each afternoon, if there was a lull between bakery customers, but after the first few days being left on his own, Tate didn't answer the ringing phone. I tried to phone you, Granny Kit said over more than one supper together at her kitchen table, but he told her each time that he had been playing outside in the yard or had gone for a bike ride around the block. She tried not to be too concerned about leaving him on his own each day. Though only eleven, he was a responsible boy, conscientious about wearing his eye patch, too. (Granny Kit doubted the eye patch would do any good at all, but she didn't want to go against his parents, especially right now.) What mattered (she believed) was that he was staying within their agreed boundaries on these afternoons. He really was such a good boy, no trouble at all.

Operation Flannagan Well Inspection consisted at first of Jane and Tate circling the Flannagans' red brick Colonial house in widening circles, starting at the foundation, then scrambling through the thicket of rhododendrons and azaleas that surrounded the house. They had gone inside the Flannagan house just once (key under back door mat) and had found it disconcertingly devoid of the usual clutter to which they were accustomed. It was practically like a movie set of a house.

Where was their personal stuff? There were only matching sets of books on a few shelves. There had been a surprising bowl of fresh red roses on the piano, but when Jane got close to smell them she discovered that they were silk flowers. No wonder they looked fresh even though the Flannagans had been away for two weeks. Tate had finally located a deep junk drawer in the laundry room, and from there they had chosen a box of wooden matches. There was a jar of old coins, from which Jane selected a very old, worn silver dime.

Next step in the inspection, they crisscrossed the front and back and side lawns, mapping the locations of the sprinkler heads that popped up every day at half past five. There were thirty-two of them. One sprinkler head near the garden shed was apparently broken; the grass in its vicinity had withered and turned yellow. As Jane and Tate moved across the Flannagans' yard, they both felt watched by the phalanx of foot-high garden gnomes lined up on one edge of the paved terrace. They added a full count and description of the gnomes to the mission's inventory.

A dozen! Why? Each gnome wore a floppy dunce cap and had a big nose. One had glasses. They were halfway between cartoon-like and sinister. They appeared to be a matched set, though one was missing the pointed top of his red dunce cap. Tate noticed that just two of the dozen only had chin beards while the rest had full beards with mustaches. It was like the Jack of Clubs, he said (Jane wrote this down, too), the only Jack without a mustache.

Tate touched one tentatively. They seemed to be made of concrete and could hardly be budged. He leaned into it until it wobbled and scraped as it moved, revealing a dark rim of paving under its black-booted feet. We're looking for the well, Jane reminded him. Neither of them knew what they were looking for, but surely there would be a clue any moment. The only well either of them could picture was the wishing well of fables and fairy tales, with a bucket on a rope.

Though it was only the middle of the afternoon, they had not noticed until now that the sky had been darkening rapidly. There was a startling wind gust. Fat drops of rain fell. They stood still for another moment and the rate of falling drops increased, and then the rain came crashing down in earnest. They heard a rumble of thunder.

Come on, Jane tugged at the hem of Tate's striped shirt. Can we get into that shed? The Flannagans had a garden shed down at the far end of their backyard, beyond their flower beds. They had peered in the dusty windows the week before, on their way to Jane's garage to incorporate the day's takings from the Pasterns' house (a goldmine of Monopoly tokens, ivory dominoes, a Twister spinner, a cup filled with several pairs of dice, and a purple velvet drawstring bag filled with Scrabble tiles—Shop without shopping! Tate had exclaimed gleefully as they made their exit), so they had not stopped for long. Neat pegboards hung with gardening tools, each with its place outlined, were discouraging for their purposes, if everything had a place and everything was in its place. Clutter was better. They had not made it a priority to go inside the Flannagans' shed. The intensity of the rain increased, like a car changing gears. The shed door wasn't locked and opened easily once Tate figured out how to use Ye Olde Colonial thumb latch, pushing down with his thumb to lever and lift the drop bar from the keeper on the inside of the door.

They were both drenched and stood there dripping in the dim shed. The thundering rain on the corrugated tin roof was deafening, and they had to shout to each other. Not that either of them had much to say just then. There was a tremendously loud crack, and almost at the same moment a dazzling flash of lightning lit up the shed for an instant, then it was dark again. They stood there companionably for another long moment and then the rain was letting up and the sky was brightening. They could see where they were. A few tendrils of sickly pale ivy had found their way inside the shed, growing through a crack between the bottom of the wall and the concrete block footings the shed sat on. The ivy had grown several feet across the floor. There was something a little creepy about it.

They don't come in here much, said Jane, recognizing that the tidy Flannagans would surely have pulled the ivy. Their pegboards full of gardening tools, each outlined like a body at a crime scene, were hung on two walls, over potting tables, which held stacks of red clay flowerpots and saucers. There was a bucket full of small wooden marker stakes for the garden, and automatically Tate scooped up a handful. Those are good, Jane said. They both looked around. What else? The sun was now actually coming out.

A crumpled blue tarpaulin covered something large in the corner. A snowblower? An old wading pool? Jane lifted one grommeted edge to flip it back and found a surprising pair of slanted doors set in a concrete foundation—she had seen these outside basement doors on some houses. B I L C O, read Tate, turning his head sideways to make out the raised lettering on the outer frame of the doors. Was the alleged well for watering their lawn behind those doors? Together, Jane and Tate dragged the tarpaulin off and bundled it onto the dirt floor. There was a padlocked bicycle chain in a clear plastic sleeve that ran through the two door handles. Without a word, Tate ran over to the stacks of terra cotta pots and saucers and began pulling them apart restacking as he went, first the pots, and then the saucers. Just as he reached the last saucers, the silvery padlock key dropped onto the table.

I wonder what latitude or longitude we've got to, whispered Jane, as they climbed down the rough, steep wooden steps that were practically like a ladder, Jane first, then Tate just above her. There was no handrail, just a rough block wall that scraped the side of her arm as she stepped carefully down one more step and then another.

I don't know what that means, said Tate, whose voice qua-
vered a little, a combination of fear and excitement.

Neither do I, Jane admitted. Just nice grand words to say.
Alice, you know?

Who?

Never mind, watch it. Don't step on my hand.

They stood together at the bottom of the stair ladder, peering around the cobwebby gloom. It was a room. A very small
room, with a low ceiling that Jane could touch with her hand
if she stretched. It smelled of raw concrete and rust. Floor
to ceiling industrial shelving lined two walls. One wall was
stacked with canned soup, canned beans, plastic dishes and
bowls, cups, folded sheets and towels (these were damp to the
touch). Rows and rows of books (so they did read, after all, or
planned to!), piles of news magazines, a carton filled with first
aid supplies (aspirin, remedies for both diarrhea and consti-
pation, eye drops, tweezers, cortisone, antifungal, and antibi-
otic creams, razors, toothbrushes, toothpaste, and a temporary
filling kit), gallon jugs of water, cartons of toilet paper, a large
red toolbox that when opened revealed neatly-arranged tools.
Next to it was a hatchet with a rusted blade, a crowbar, and a
sledgehammer.

The other wall held rows of clear plastic boxes filled with
folded clothing. There were three blue tarpaulins still in their
packaging, surprisingly heavy and dense to move. Jane realized the fourth blue tarpaulin was the covering that had con-
cealed the entrance to this secret place. There was a shelf with
nothing but board games—dozens of flat rectangular boxes,
all sealed in their original plastic film, every board game Jane
and Tate had ever heard of and some they had never heard
of. There were six pristine decks of playing cards, still in
their wrappers. A hand-cranked radio sat beside four identical flashlights and a battery lantern on a card table. Under
the table there were two metal stools, one stacked over the

other. Also under the card table was a large plastic tub with a lid holding batteries for the lantern and flashlights, sealed in their blister packaging.

There were two canvas camp cots stacked together on their sides, black mold spots spawning in all directions on the beige canvas. In the corner there was a contraption that looked like an exercise bicycle that was attached to a shiny fat coiled pipe which hung down from the ceiling. It sat beside what seemed to be a sandbox in the corner. There was a short-handled spade stuck into the sand. (It was too sharp and heavy to be a sandbox toy. What was this for?) Everything was coated with a thin layer of gritty dust.

The only light came from above their heads, where the Bilco doors were splayed open, and the bit of daylight inside the shed was fading.

What is this place? Tate asked in a tiny voice, taking her hand for a moment and then letting go, suddenly self-conscious. Jane was touched by the way he counted on her to know things. Usually she did, though not as often as he believed.

Definitely a Flannagan operation. Jane told Tate they needed to come back with the notebook to write down a thorough inventory. No way to remember everything.

There's definitely no well down here, Tate whispered back.

Noted. They are criminal lawn-waterers. Shhhh, wait, do you hear that? Jane found herself putting her hand to her ear like an illustration in a book of someone trying to hear a sound. What is that? Is someone there? They stood frozen, not breathing.

There was indeed a definite sound. What was it? Familiar is what it was. *Chup-chup-chup-chup-ssssss-chup-chup-chup-chup-ssssss.* The illicit Flannagan sprinklers.

Over the following days, Jane and Tate moved their precious hoard, cigar box by cigar box, down into their new headquarters. The floor was damp and gritty, but The Coca-Cola crate, each compartment filled, required both of them to carry it, and even so it was an awkward task. They made this perilous final transfer moving in a synchronized crab-like trot across the open lawns between Jane's garage and the Flannagans' shed, and then the transfer was complete.

Together they wrote a list of the contents of each shelf. It seemed like an important task, a responsible thing to do if they were the new stewards of whatever this place was. They worked together, Tate standing at the shelves describing, Jane sitting at the card table writing. It dawned on her that there were no books or clothing for children. No baby formula. No diapers. A secret hiding place for grownups only.

Jane set out to make a list of the books on the shelves, but she soon realized it was a huge and actually somewhat point-less task. Instead, she decided it would be sufficient if they simply listed the numbers of books by category. Along with novels and biographies, there were almanacs and many other practical books on gardening, animal track identification, recognizing birds of North America, and a large number of titles such as how to build a log cabin, how to build a geo-desic dome, how to catch fish, how to teach yourself Espe-ranto. There were several pamphlets held together by a brittle rubber band that broke into pieces when Jane tried to pull it down. These had titles like How to Survive an Atomic Attack and How to Build a Family Fallout Shelter and If an Attack Comes, Are You Prepared?

The most significant book on these shelves, however, was none of these. It was a small, dog-eared paperback with crumbling and yellowed pages, called *HOYLE'S RULES OF GAMES*.

Jane read from the title page: Play According to Hoyle. Descriptions of Indoor Games of Skill and Chance, with Advice on Skillful Play.

So who is this Hoyle? Tate asked.

Someone who knew a lot of rules. Or made them all up. Or

both. This is great! Jane began to read from the table of contents: Accordion, Acey-Deucey, All Fours, Arlington—

I get it! You don't have to read them all.

She couldn't stop, in love with these words and all the possibilities they represented. Worlds within worlds. Human Croquet, Forty Thieves, Puss in the Corner, Liar Dice, Seven-Toed Pete, Scat, Smudge, Oh Hell, Spit-in-the-Ocean! Jane continued giddily, skipping through the list of fantastic names for all these unknown games of skill and chance. Shoot the Moon!

All these rules for all these games! An infinity of rules for Blink! They had found their Rosetta Stone, Jane told Tate, who nodded as if he knew what that was.

They sat together, side by side at the card table, taking turns finding new rules, new names for things, new procedures, one taking notes and the other reading out loud from the precious book.

Backgammon playing pieces may be termed checkers, draughts, stones, men, counters, pawns, discs, pips, chips, or nips.

Bobtail straight! Cockeyes! Spit in the ocean!

The proper card shuffling technique: Riffle riffle box riffle shuffle bridge waterfall. This was familiar, though they hadn't known the terms. It took practice. Jane could do it already. Tate could not. When he tried for the bridge, the cards sprayed out of his hands every time.

One-eyed Jacks have the option to be wild, Jane read out. Sometimes she forgot that Tate wore an eye patch. She looked over the book at him. Are you a wild one-eyed Jack?

Jack of Spades and Jack of Hearts are the one-eyed Jacks, Tate offered. (The things he knew.) Hearts. I'll be the Jack of Hearts. He was grateful that Jane had never once said Ahoy Matey or asked for his pegleg and parrot.

I know why pirates wear a patch on one eye, he told Jane.

Not because they lost an eye?

No. Well, maybe, sometimes, but my vision therapist told me that if one eye is in the dark all the time, then if the pirate has to go down below deck where it's dark, or if they have to go into a cave or something, if that's where the pirate booty is hidden, then they can just lift up the patch and that eye will already be adjusted to see in the dark.

A wild one-eyed Jack could be any card in the deck, could be anything.

Unlike Jane's garage, where they had to put everything away at the end of each Blink session, down here in Blink HQ (as they had decided to call this secret room) they could leave all the boards and playing pieces (there were now four additional boards from the games on the shelves added to the playing field, which practically covered the entire floor of the shelter) set up, ready to resume business where they had left off the day before. They hardly rode their bicycles anymore, and had curtailed their scouting missions, skipping days and heading right to the shed unless they needed something specific for Blink enhancement, preferring to spend their afternoons in their underground fortress of solitude. They were both so easily lost in the depths of Blink that only near-darkness alerted them to the lateness of the hour most afternoons. Tate had to scramble more than once to get home ahead of his grandmother.

Though it was possible to see in the dim light that filtered down through the open hatch doors from the shed interior above, they had grown accustomed to using the flashlights and battery lantern, switching out the used-up batteries for fresh ones when the lights dimmed. Their supply of batteries was running low, because almost half of the batteries in the tub were corroded and leaking. They began a new kind of mission: taking used batteries into the houses up and down the street and swapping them for the fresh ones they found in drawers and cupboards. People might notice if their battery supply had vanished, but if the batteries they thought were new turned out to be used up, most people would just shrug and buy new ones, choosing a better brand this time, one that wouldn't go dead just sitting in a drawer.

The food supplies on the shelves were beyond consideration, but perhaps they should borrow some cans and jars of their own from the variety of pantries on the street which they knew very well. They wrote a list of what they needed. They argued about the pronunciation of the word "victuals," which both had seen in books and neither had ever heard said aloud, and so finally they settled on "provisions."

They were getting close to starting their first Blink session, but first Tate had decided they needed to add more spots on some of the old white dominoes (according to Hoyle the proper word was "pips") to create higher denominations. He also marked pips on some of the smooth flat poker chips they had collected from three different houses. The plastic dominoes gave off toxic fumes when burned by the tip of the woodburning tool, but he was only marking dots, so it wasn't intolerable. This he did with great skill, in Jane's garage, where they needed an outlet for the woodburning tool, which had an old-fashioned round plug at the end of its cloth-covered cord. Pyrography. Writing with fire, the instructions explained. Of course, they could have set the place on fire, and this could have led to a tragic inferno, but that didn't happen.

Would you make me a card? Jane asked Tate during one of their timeless subterranean Blink afternoons.

With your name on it, like a business card?

No, I mean with scissors and glue. Something to match the Jack. We need it for Blink. Right now it's as if there are four cards missing from each deck. The King and the Queen are a pair. But there is only a Jack in the four royal families. Why is the Jack an only child? Wasn't the Queen once somebody's daughter? It's not right. There should be Janes to go with the Jacks.

Sacrificing one of the fresh decks from the shelves, he cut the Queen of Hearts free from her four framing Qs and glued her onto the Jack of Hearts, covering the Jack precisely to make a Jane of Hearts, a gift she'd earned. They decided he didn't need to make Janes of Spades or Diamonds or Clubs for now. Jane of Hearts was the only Jane, a match for the Wild Jack of Hearts, the perfect pair.

They explored the mysteries of the secret room a little more, curious about the stationary bike that was so rusted the wheel would hardly turn, even when Tate stood on the pedals. It seemed to be set up to turn a wheel in a housing that powered a fan blade that blew air up the flexible chute that vented to the outside of the shed. It was a ventilation system of sorts. Jane had secretly taken home one of the survival pamphlets to read without Tate, and now she knew why there was a sandbox in the corner. It was a giant litterbox for people. It was the bathroom. This was disconcerting. The mysterious lawnproud Flannagans had apparently made a plan to hide down here for a long time. But that tub of batteries, corroded or not, wouldn't have lasted very long, and with the doors above closed against whatever doomy thing the Flannagans planned to hide from, they would have been spooning their canned soup and using their sandbox in utter darkness. Jane did not want to think about any of this, but mental pictures kept coming to mind, unbidden.

Each day, Jane and Tate practiced their secret two-note whistle. Their Blink whistle. They made an illogical plan to use it in case of a total Blink HQ blackout, without consideration for the fact that they would be only a few feet apart from each other. What if somebody came along and closed the hatch and locked them in? The Blink whistle signal would do little good if they were locked in together. (Shouting would be more effective.) The two whistles together echoed brightly in the little space, like singing in the bathtub.

A jar of fireflies for backup, Tate proposed. But such bioluminescent illumination would only last a day.

It was getting dark a little earlier each day.

A horrifying development. One of the partners at Jane's mother's office, Fred Barker, was on the board of a wilderness adventure program for teens. (The very word "teens" coming from her mother was agonizing to Jane.) Given that this summer vacation had an extra week, with Labor Day coming so late, there was an opportunity. Jane was signed up for an Expedition Leadership five-night wilderness trip. The delicious roast history chicken her mother had brought home (Jane recognized this for the bribe it was) sat on her plate, untouched, as Jane tried to say no thank you to this unexpected opportunity as her mother kept calling it. There had been a cancellation when some poor girl came down with mono. The trip was being given to her, wasn't this generous of Mr. Barker? (Mr. Barker was divorced and he liked Jane's mother. It wasn't clear to Jane if her mother was divorced.) There was a brochure with pictures of happy smiling teens in helmets suspended in space as they rappelled a cliff face. There was a checklist of everything she would need—only two t-shirts!—and her mother had already organized most of it.

Her mother said she felt guilty that Jane had spent most of the summer in the great indoors.

I rode my bike, Jane protested.

She knew that, her mother told her, but not very far, and it was sweet that she had been willing to spend so much time with that boy with the eye patch staying with his grandmother, Kitty who worked behind the counter at Lorraine's, but this was going to be a great adventure, a wonderful way to prepare for seventh grade at her new school.

Jane felt sick. The bus to Brattleboro would pick her up in the church parking lot at eight in the morning, day after next.

Jane and Tate sat on the front steps of Granny Kit's house. Jane had gone there after dinner to tell him this terrible news. Granny Kit had been surprised by her appearance on the other side of the screen door, but she brought them each a slice of flakey apple strudel (which children rarely like as much as grownups think they do) and left them alone.

I have to go, Jane said grimly.

What will I do? Tate asked. We were almost ready to start our Blink tournament. He looked as if he were about to cry. She put her arm around his shoulder tentatively, and he leaned in. Jane felt fiercely protective of her little assistant, and she was upset on his behalf as much as she didn't want to go on this trip because she just knew she hated things like this, not that she had ever experienced more than a one-night Brownie sleep-out in a backyard tent. She had hated sleeping on the ground, and she had hated the mildew smell in the tent, which she could taste every time she inhaled, but at least Tina had been there too, and they had giggled and complained about it together afterwards. She wouldn't know anyone. She was unprepared. If only Tina was going on the Expedition Leadership trip (which Expedition Leadership called a Quest in their brochure)! Jane had not felt the urgent missing of the Bartletts since the Blink HQ preoccupation had eclipsed all other interests in recent days.

It's only five nights. You'll hold down the fort, Jane told him.

The hiking was exhausting; the mosquito bites were annoying; there were breakfasts of scorched, raw pancakes they cooked on little stoves they made from coffee cans (this felt pointless to Jane—she could see the frying pans!); and there were songs and shivery ghost stories around a campfire each night; and the rappelling was frightening at first, but then Jane had felt triumphant when she managed to do it well, better than some of the others. The Expedition guides, two college sophomores from Maine, were relentlessly cheerful. Some of the girls in the group were nice, potential friends even, though Jane would probably never see them again, since two of them were from New York City, three were from a suburb of Boston, and the rest of them all went to school together in Greenwich, which wasn't actually that far from Northbury, but Jane knew, and the girls knew, that it was a world away. As it was, the Expedition Leadership adventure was itself a world away from Northbury and the secret world Jane and Tate had made in the Flannagans' underground bunker.

From the bus window, Jane looked out at her mother's old Volvo wagon in the church parking lot. As she got off the bus, the Greenwich girls chorused their goodbyes, claiming they would invite her to a reunion sleepover one weekend soon. Jane could feel them watching her as she clambered awkwardly down the steep steps to the pavement, encumbered by the bulk of her backpack and the dangling stuff sack holding her sleeping bag. Her mother got out of the car and opened the tailgate, and Jane felt guilty for her relief that the Greenwich girls' glimpse of her mother in jeans and a pretty blue shirt, with her hair swept back, had no cringe potential. (Some weekends, when Jane's mother wore tattered leggings and embroidered peasant blouses, with a bandana tied around her head like a bandage, she looked like a crazy aging hippie.)

On the short drive home, Jane's mother told her there was news. Some of the families on their street had come back from vacation, and it seemed there had been break-ins while they were away.

Like burglaries you mean, Jane said nervously, looking away from her mother out the car window, surfing the force of the air current with her outstretched hand.

Maybe. Not exactly. Her mother hesitated. I don't want to exaggerate this. Nothing big, only little things. Nobody is really sure, and there were no broken windows or forced doors, as far as the police can tell.

Police? Police!

Yes, but the police don't really have anything to investigate. Maybe some homeless person was just looking for a place to go. It's mysterious. Or it was kids. But what kids? It was quiet, nobody heard any cars. I certainly didn't hear anything. The Dishers were home, and they never heard or saw anything.

Jane waited for her mother to say more. Where was Tate right now? What was he doing and where was he doing it? She felt sick. How did they think they could get away with all of it?

One of the reasons they had not yet commenced their Blink tournament was the unresolved definition of winning. The scoring was elaborate, involving many tallies and counts and awarded stars and forfeitures, and collections of pieces in designated patterns to be fulfilled—but without a finish line to cross, without a delineated path to a victorious conclusion, how could there be a winner who takes all? They had not worked this out. How would the game end? Would the game ever end?

You and that boy with the eye patch, Tate? When you were riding your bicycles in the neighborhood, did you and that boy ever see anything, anyone suspicious?

We were only riding around the block, Jane said. He isn't allowed to go anywhere else. His grandmother won't let him.

Not everyone on our street is back from vacation yet, but so far, the break-ins were only on our street, up and down both sides, almost every house. The police are going door-to-door, checking. You never saw anyone you didn't know, a strange car?

The Amway lady.

Her mother laughed. The Amway lady is not a suspect.

How can you be sure? It would be the perfect disguise for a burglar! Jane said defensively. They should definitely investigate the Amway lady!

You're very imaginative. Don't get carried away. There was one possible sighting of this thief. The Bartletts—Tina was looking for you, she'll be glad you're back—came home right after you left, the next day. When they were unloading the car, they thought they heard someone in the house.

What do you mean? Jane felt a thump of terror.

They think someone was in their house—Melissa heard the back door closing. There was a drawer open in the kitchen.

Jane sat very still, her heart pounding. (She was impatient when characters in books feel their hearts pounding as a way for the author to add to the suspense and drama, but now it was actually happening.) But did they see anyone? she asked as casually as she could, hoping she sounded merely curious and not like someone with everything at stake.

No, they didn't. By the time Melissa told her parents, and by the time they saw the pulled-out drawer, whoever it was had plenty of time to get away. You can cut across to Hawthorn Street if you go over that low fence and walk through the Peets' backyard.

When was this? Jane could see Tate running for his life, scrambling over that fence they had climbed together numerous times. She had taught him that short-cut to the other side of the block.

I just told you, it was right after you left, the next day.

Jane hardly knew where to begin. She would need to make a list. Why hadn't she forbidden Tate from making any solo missions? He probably thought she would be pleased. What a disaster. She would go look for Tate, right after lunch.

Another strange thing happened while you were camping, and I do want to hear all about your trip, especially the rappelling, and the other girls, Jane's mother told her (over their tuna sandwiches and potato chips, with the sweet pickles Jane liked best). This was just a couple of days ago. You know Kitty, who worked at Lorraine's? Of course you do, that boy with the eye patch—you know who I mean—

Tate.

Tate, yes, he's her grandson.

Jane waited apprehensively. Sure, Granny Kit. What about her?

It's the oddest thing, the Fischers just won't say why or tell anyone what she did. But she's not working at Lorraine's anymore.

What? Why? They fired her? What do you mean, what she did?

I don't know. It's mysterious. It's not clear if they fired her or if she quit. They aren't accusing her of anything officially, but they're saying she wasn't honest.

Sentence first, verdict afterwards?

Exactly, her mother said. Off with her head!

This was not good.

Because of the mysterious break-ins just one block over, and who knew how many more would be discovered once everyone returned from holidays, Tate's grandmother had not wanted to leave him alone in the house while she was at the bakery, so after taking some days off from work in order to keep an eye on him (he moped around the house until she let him go outside to circle the block on his mother's blue bicycle for a while, but those days had dragged for him as if time had actually stopped), she had insisted that he go to Lorraine's with her, very much against his protests that he would be fine on his own.

Granny Kit told him she had been wrong to leave him

unsupervised all those afternoons, and they could count their lucky stars nothing had gone wrong. Most little boys would not complain about being forced to spend an afternoon or two at a bakery, she told him. No arguments. You can bring a book.

Tate had sat dutifully with a book in his lap on the bench in front of Lorraine's window, where people often sat while savoring the first bites of whatever buttery, flakey pastry they had chosen from the glass cases. After two hours of inter-mittent attempts at blurry, slow reading (why had he grabbed from Granny Kit's shelf this heavy volume of *Treasure Island*, with its minuscule type instead of bringing *The Borrowers Afield*, which Jane had lent to him?), he had gone inside the bakery, thirsty and in need of a bathroom. The bell over the door jingled as he walked in, and Mrs. Fischer beamed her usual welcome, which evaporated from her face when she saw that it was only Tate. The Fischers didn't like children very much, despite all their smiles and feigned interest in birthdays and flavor preferences and remembering which child didn't like coconut (most children) and which child always wanted a birthday pie instead of a birthday cake. Mrs. Fischer had no choice but to agree that of course he could use the bakery bathroom, even though it was for employees only.

Granny Kit directed him to the bathroom, which was through a side door to a connecting passage leading to the stairs up to their apartment. The cramped bathroom was a windowless cubicle converted from a coat closet (it had been required when new health and safety codes had been intro-duced, after Lorraine's had been doing a thriving business for a decade). There was just space for the toilet and the smallest sink Tate had ever seen, mounted in the corner. (He had never flown on a plane or he would have noted the similarity to an airplane bathroom.)

A short moment later he had returned, distressed, because

the light bulb overhead had blown when he pulled the string. Tate was afraid to leave the bathroom door open in this strange place (he was a modest child), and he was afraid to close it and shut himself into complete blackness that even his pirate eye couldn't penetrate. Reluctantly, Olga Fischer directed him up the stairs to use the bathroom in their apartment. She was in no mood for a needless walk up the steep stairs with her bad knees, and the timers were going off on several racks of viennoiserie proofing, which she didn't trust Kitty to manage correctly, so she sent him on his own.

Of course, despite the very close call the day before when the Bartletts had come home while he was in their kitchen, Tate had wandered through the rooms of the Fischers' apartment after he used the bathroom (which was luxuriously bright and spacious, compared to the tiny employee cubicle downstairs). It was stuffy in their apartment, as if the thick, jewel-toned velvet upholstery and carpets and draperies absorbed all fresh air and sounds from the outside world. An ornate clock with a gold face sat on a marble-topped table, which amplified its ticking.

The Fischers had many precious things they treasured. There were miniature painted foxes in various poses, which were quite heavy (they were made of lead), and ornately decorated eggs on carved stands (these were counterfeit Faberge eggs for which Olga's mother had paid too much, a misjudgment, a bad investment). There were six delicate porcelain parrots (German Sitzendorf porcelains inherited from Stefan Fischer's mother, who hid them under the floorboards in her Budapest apartment during the war). On Mrs. Fischer's dressing table, which was littered with an array of appealing, takeable items, Tate selected just one, which he stuffed deep into the front pocket of his pants: a small, hand-sewn pincushion, made to look like a tomato, complete with green felt leaves at the top.

Of course, Tate had no way to know that this small stuffed tomato (he didn't know it was a pincushion and he didn't know what a pincushion was, even though this one was studded with a dozen pins, pushed in all the way to their colored ball tops) held a valuable secret. It had been made with care by Olga's mother. It was one of three identical pincushions she had sewn for her three daughters after their father died.

When Olga's father was discharged from the Bolshevik army in the autumn of 1918, he limped his way back to Kuznetsovsk, his home village. He walked with a limp for the rest of his life. He had been shot in the foot, and the wound became infected in the primitive military hospital in Yekaterinburg, where he had run a very high fever and almost died, but he was young, and very strong. Sergei never spoke about the ordeal, which nearly cost him his foot, if not his entire leg. He told only one person, Olga's mother Katerina—on their wedding night—about the day he was wounded. This was his story:

Sergei had been one of two dozen soldiers in the detail guarding a "house of special purpose." He was there for many weeks but had never crossed the threshold, and had never seen the prisoner inhabitants of Ipatiev House until the night of July 16th, when he was one of a dozen soldiers brought inside and stationed in a basement hallway, guns drawn. They had been issued a ragtag assortment of weaponry, and at the last moment he had traded with one of his comrades, swapping his thirty-year-old Nagant pistol in exchange for what he knew was a better pistol, a twenty-year-old Mauser.

They stood there silently in the hallway, ready for action, sweating in their heavy uniforms, waiting and waiting some more for the next order. Seven soldiers were given orders to advance, and then each was given a specific order, while the rest were kept back.

There was a sudden fusillade of gunfire in an adjacent room, a deafening, thunderous barrage accompanied by piercing screams. The gunfire stopped for a moment, but the screaming did not, and then there was a second long volley of gunshots. The air was thick with the smell of gunpowder. The screaming finally died away. Sergei's group were ordered to holster their weapons. Still they stood there in the dim hallway.

Finally, they were ordered to go into that small room to assist with the cleaning up. There he saw, through the clearing gun smoke, the bloody, mutilated corpses of the Tsar, his wife, and their five children, their white clothing soaked nearly black with blood, their faces butchered beyond recognition. They had been shot repeatedly, some had been bayoneted. Sergei was certain he could see two of the girls still breathing.

Under instructions being barked by the commanding officer, who seemed drunk, some of the soldiers were stripping the corpses down to the skin to find every single jewel that had been sewn inside the clothing of every member of the Imperial Romanov family. They were so armored with their hidden Imperial jewels, so laden with kilos of gold and diamonds and exquisite gem-crusted necklaces and brooches, that most of the first fusillade had failed to penetrate this armor. This was why it had taken so long to murder them.

After the bodies had been rolled up in military sheets and carried out on stretchers—a single deafening gunshot made everyone jump when one of the daughters moved her arm and the drunk officer held his Mauser to her head and shot her, and blood was everywhere—Sergei was assigned the task of collecting and counting all the bullets on the floor and embedded in the blood-spattered wall. This he had done. He had also discovered that any number of loose diamonds were there for the taking, lying at the edge of the skirting board, glinting in the cracks between the floorboards, sticky with blood. Nobody else had yet noticed. As he crawled on the floor searching for bullets, his head low, he picked up as many of these diamonds as he could, swallowing them like medi-cine tablets, trying not to taste the blood, gulping them down, one after the other.

Who is to say if every aspect of this story is true? Was Sergei in the group of soldiers who cleaned up and hunted for bullets, as he said, or was he actually among the seven soldiers chosen to enter that room first, guns drawn, each ordered to aim and shoot and aim and shoot again and until the assigned family member was dead?

And how did Sergei get shot, ending his days as a soldier in the Bolshevik Army? He was cleaning his Mauser that same evening when he accidentally shot himself in the foot.

The pincushion Tate put in his pocket had three of those diamonds at its center. They were the last of Olga's heritage, her dowry, her legacy. There had been more, divided equally among Sergei's three daughters, but over the years Olga's diamonds had paid for many needed things, steamship passage and bakery equipment and the purchase of the bakery build-ing. This was truly heritage. Sergei, too, had sold a diamond to pay for the construction of a very fine domed brick bread oven for his bakery in Kuznetsovsk. They were very fine diamonds.

When, late that night, they noticed that the pincushion was gone, the Fischers drove to Kitty Welch's house. It was nearly midnight, and Tate was woken by the sound of their raised voices coming from the kitchen. He sat on the stairs to lis-ten, and after the words "tomato" and "pincushion" had been repeated, he understood that he had taken something of far greater value than he could possibly have imagined. Why on earth, he heard Granny Kit say, is this pincushion so impor-tant you drove here at midnight instead of phoning, or even better, waiting until morning?

They needed it back. They needed it now. He scrambled

back to bed when he heard the kitchen chairs all scraping.
Even when his grandmother came into his room and turned
on the light and asked him if he knew anything about this
tomato pincushion, even when the Fischers who had followed
her up the stairs burst in behind her and began ransacking his
room in a frenzy, dumping out drawers and pulling books off
the shelves, demanding that he return the tomato pincushion
immediately, he played the part of the sleepy confused child
who had no idea what they were talking about.

Finally, they departed, speaking rapidly to each other
in another language. In English, Stefan said they said they
would be back. Fortunately, the item in question was not in
the house at all. Earlier that evening, while his grandmother
was making dinner, Tate had bicycled around the block and
had made a crucial stop. But now he knew what he had to do
first thing in the morning.

Jane had meant to wake up early and meet up with Tate, but
her mother was on vacation and had not set an alarm, and
they both slept late. Over breakfast, Jane's mother asked if
she had mentioned that the Flannagans had come home from
Nantucket, and while they didn't think anyone had been in
their house, they thought their garden shed might have been
broken into. What a sad thing, if people had to start locking
everything up?

Had Tate been down in Blink HQ? Had he placed the blue
tarpaulin back over the Bilco doors exactly as they had first
found it, the way they always did together each time? This
was very bad. What if the Flannagans put an actual lock on
the shed?

When Jane knocked on the door, and then rang, there was
only silence at Tate's grandmother's house. Granny Kit's car
was not there. She rang the doorbell again and called through
the letter slot in case Tate was home but not answering the

door, per the rules. She walked around to the back and peered in through the wavy glass panes in the back door at the inert kitchen. There was a stillness, a blankness to the house that she could feel. She decided to bicycle down the street to check for any sign of a Flannagan return.

There were four landscapers in gray uniforms working at the Flannagans'. Their big mowers were on a trailer parked on the street out in front, and the lawn had been freshly cut. The door to the garden shed stood open. As Jane watched from across the street, drenched in doom, perched on her bicycle, one foot on the sidewalk edge for balance, she saw that they were dragging blue tarpaulins out of the shed. They were heaped with books and cans and boxes. In one, she could see the weird stationary bicycle on its side, trailing the long vent tube which had ripped open, like an exposed giant Slinky. The men hoisted the laden tarps and carried them across the lawn, to heave up into the back of a pickup truck. One of them stood in the truck, pulling each plastic sheet, and then all four returned to the shed, dragging the tarpaulins back across the grass. A breeze lifted one like a sail, and it flapped for a moment before one of the landscapers grabbed the corner that had blown from his grasp.

Jane was hollow with sorrow. Everything was gone. This was what it must have felt like for Pod and Homily and Arrietty when Crampfurl the gardener pulled up the floorboard and stirred everything—all their furnishings, all their possessions—with his ignorant boot. If only Tate were here, perched on his bicycle beside her, Jane would have said All that's missing now is the boy with a ferret. But Tate wasn't there, or anywhere.

Tate and his grandmother had moved away suddenly. Precipitously. Nobody knew where they had gone. Someone thought

Chicago. The one place in the world Jane knew Tate would not be found. Soon after Labor Day, while Jane was at her new school, which wasn't so bad, a moving van appeared and three men methodically emptied Granny Kit's house. When asked, the movers didn't know anything more than the destination for the load: storage. A "For Sale" sign was planted on the lawn soon after that. A family from Texas with twin toddlers moved in just before Christmas.

Jane, of course, didn't yet know any of this when she slowly pedaled home, but she had begun to know with certainty that she would never see Tate again, not if his father's trial was over and now they were going to go live their secret new lives somewhere new and secret. When she wheeled her bicycle into the garage to put it away, something caught her eye in the far corner, the spot where she and Tate had begun their Blink empire in a cigar box, and then another, and then in the Coca-Cola crate. There was a single cigar box, a Partagas box, tucked almost entirely out of sight, behind the blade of the cracked plastic snow shovel. The plaid notebook was on top of it. Holding the notebook, Jane lifted the lid.

Inside this box, using Dr. van Dycks' woodburning tool (which was here too, in its cigar box, next to the bucket of rusty trowels), Tate had painstakingly inscribed JANE at the top and HEARTS at the bottom. The Jane of Hearts card he had made for her with scissors and glue lay in the center, covering the OF. Here was the heart-shaped green shard of sea glass. (They had argued pointlessly one afternoon about whether drift glass and sea glass were the same thing. Now Jane couldn't remember which side she had taken. For the rest of her life she would try to recall Tate's preference.) Here were tokens for essential Blink moves: Marbles, a key, Tate's first red poker chip, coins of the realms, a Monopoly house, Mrs. Bartlett's lipstick. And three diamonds.

I remember the whole beginning as a succession of flights and drops, a little seesaw of the right throbs and the wrong. Are those words familiar? I am a thief and I have stolen them from Henry James as I describe those secret summer days forty years ago, when windows became mirrors for a pair of children to pass through.

The truth is: These events did or did not occur. Tate is alive and he is also dead. There is no record of any little boy known as Tate Baldwin, not the eleven-year-old then, not the fifty-year-old he would be now. At the end of that summer he vanished. No living person I know remembers him. There may, of course, be ordinary explanations for this. People get lost all the time. Was the circumstance of his stay with his grandmother in Northbury, Connecticut embellished for dramatic effect by a ridiculously active imagination? Did he misoverhear? Does he rarely look back on that interlude from a humdrum existence somewhere, with only the dimmest recollection, or does he often recall the events of those days vividly, despite the intervening years? Was his story of his father's dangerous testimony genuine, or was it the product of a boy's wild inventiveness?

Either way, it is as impossible to let him go as it is impossible to keep him. In the end, we were nothing but a pack of cards, he and I—and some cigar boxes full of children's treasures. All of this happened and none of it's true. Or maybe none of this happened and all of it's true. I am, after all, rather easily carried away.